Through the Eyes
of a Vulture

B. Mikitowicz

ISBN: 978-0-9915374-7-1

DEDICATION

<u>These stories are dedicated to:</u>

My grandparents, Walter and Mildred Mikitowicz.

Barry. I'm kidding, I would *never* do that.

My true love, my wife, Hannah.

Most of all, to my mother, Suzanne Mikitowicz Kuehn.
Without her, these stories never would have been possible.

CONTENTS

In the Shadow of a Vulture

B. Mikitowicz

PROLOGUE
BEFORE THE VULTURE

Jack was the third and youngest child of Lenard and Carol Chestnut. His father was a project manager at a local construction firm, where he publicly blamed his thinning hair on his children. Dad coached both Jack's and his older brother, Joey's, recreational soccer teams. Lenard was extremely generous with his advice, sharing it with anyone who would listen—most often, his youngest boy, Jack. Much of the time, Lenard's guidance was quite sage. Unfortunately, Jack was too young to grasp the totality of his father's wisdom. Regardless, Lenard enjoyed the attention.

One Christmas morning, after beating young Jack at the family's new, electric slot-car racetrack, Lenard victoriously stated, "Races aren't won at the finish line, son. They're won at every turn before it. Now, pick up your jockstrap. We're going to be late for church." Jack was three years old and had no idea what a jockstrap was.

They had a family barbecue every year in June. That year, Lenard told Jack, "Don't forget that if you live your life like the person you want to be perceived as, in the end, you'll be remembered exactly as that ideal self that you always strived for." Jack looked blankly at his father and wiped his tongue

3

across his vanilla ice cream cone. Lenard stood up and straightened his back. Next, he tended the grill, and gave a holler to Carol, "Baby! What happened to my beer? It's hotter than South Texas out here and this grill is like a dragon blowing on my balls."

"Dad! Gross!" shouted C.C., holding her ice cream cone away from her mouth.

C.C. preferred her initials to her full name, Cynthia Carol Chestnut, and everyone respected that. She was the middle child of the Chestnut family, and also Jack's best confidant. She was someone who truly listened to his dreams. While their parents and older brother, Joey, were flipping through TV channels, C.C. and Jack would play hide-and-go-seek or lay outside in the yard and try to make shapes out of the clouds. They were best friends, and she always looked out for Jack and gave him advice he could actually use.

The following year, shortly before the next family barbecue, Lenard and C.C. died in a car accident on the way home from her dance recital.

The family changed overnight. Carol had to get a job and re-enroll at Daytona Beach Community College. Joey, the oldest brother, began entering competitive eating contests to help pay the bills. Little Jack started sleeping much more than he used to.

When he was six-and-a-half years old, Jack began drawing pictures of his dreams. He colored his first drawing of Wings, the girl he met in one of those dreams, with a small pack of Crayola crayons. The picture was of them together on an Olympic platform diving board, in the center of the Super Dome. The seats were full of spectators. Below the diving board, the Ghostbusters were battling Emperor Palpatine from Star Wars, while Godzilla fought the 'Stay Puft' Marshmallow Man. After closely reviewing the art, Carol called the piece "very busy" and smiled at her youngest son.

Carol worked hard to raise her two remaining children. She loved to laugh, but didn't tell many jokes, and avoided talking about her personal life with strangers. She began to wear oversized, dark sunglasses because even years after the accident she would find herself instantly overwhelmed and in tears. Jack remembered the day she stopped cutting the crusts off his peanut butter and jelly sandwiches—she was wearing those infamous shades.

By the time he turned sixteen, Joey already looked and acted like an adult. He worked an overnight shift at Springhill Suites, a local hotel, and completed his homework in the downtime. He put in nearly forty hours a week and contributed his earnings and eating contest winnings toward the monthly bills. Carol initially dissuaded him, but Joey insisted that he was doing it to make his father proud. Once again, tears escaped from behind Carol's thick glasses, as she accepted her son's assistance. This was the day Joey started acting like he was Jack's boss.

Jack was the little brother in both size and age. He rejected Joey as the man of the house because he felt that he was a man, too. Joey played football, baseball, and golf in high school. So, Jack focused on soccer, basketball, and ran cross-country as an act of rebellion.

Jack learned about women by watching romantic comedies and action movies. This was a big mistake. Soon, he found out that solely liking extremely beautiful, sophisticated, and charming women severely limited his options – not to mention that trying to win those few girls over by simply being a nice guy with little to offer had an astronomical rate of failure in the real world.

Consequently, Jack was a virgin when he started college at Florida State University. Then, he met Emily. The two were inseparable. They had planned to study together in Italy. Since she was a virgin too, Jack planned to propose to her in Florence. Their relationship ended abruptly when Jack discovered that Emily was lying about being a virgin, complaining about Jack's virginity to her sorority sisters, and having real sex with her ex-boyfriend from high school. It devastated Jack. He went to Italy alone, still a virgin.

Europe changed the course of Jack's life. In Paris, he had his first legal beer. It tasted of freedom, respect, and peace of mind. Two days later, he lost his virginity to a German girl, named Martina, whom he met on a train headed to the Erlangen Beer Festival in Mannheim.

By the time Jack got to Florence for school, he never wanted to go home. The first night of their study abroad program, Jack met his future best friend, Dustin Switch, at a local pub.

"Hey, Chief. Can I bum a cigarette?" Dustin casually asked Jack.

"Bum?" Jack quickly replied in disbelief, "Dude, are you actually indigent? It's not like its one in the morning and you're out of cigarettes and cash. It's happy hour! Look, the sun is still out. Shit, I'm standing here at the bar because I haven't even ordered my first beer yet! Bro, you need to go buy a pack of fucking smokes." Jack shook his head, then reluctantly removed a cigarette, added the caveat, "Don't ask me again," in disgust, and handed it over. Naturally, the two instantly hated one another.

Dustin had never met his father, but his mom was born wealthy and he never went without. He became a member of the Screen Actors Guild and dropped out of college after his first major movie role in King Klaws. Horror movies became Dustin's gravy train. His obnoxious bravado got him on the fast track to big screen mutilation.

After Italy, Jack spent the rest of college finding new places to live, work, and go to school, outside of the United States. He wasn't openly religious, but after a year of working as a middle school social studies and theology teacher back in Daytona, he decided to keep the Ten Commandments close to heart, just in case. Jack loved to whistle, and he often had a book to read because he didn't enjoy just standing around doing nothing or talking to strangers. He wore a sweatband on his arm that doubled as a beer koozie, and several rubber bands on his wrist, which he used judiciously.

Jack had many bank accounts and little money: Italy (15.12 EUR), Australia (5.23 AUD), Switzerland (0.90 CHF), London (112.00 GBP), and United States (1,512.45 USD). He was about to take his life's savings and move to Greece for the fall, but he hadn't bought the plane ticket.

In the end, Jack wanted to be a famous artist and author, but he was not. He also wanted a girlfriend, but he didn't have one. Other than that, he was somewhat content. When he moved to London, he initially shared a two-bedroom apartment with seven other people from different countries. He mostly kept to himself.

By Wednesday, August 11th, 2006, all of Jack's flatmates were gone or had moved out for the summer except for Bridget. She was a hairdresser, and Jack found her quite attractive. Dustin was in town visiting his current girlfriend, Carrie. Jack's older brother had a full-time job and was about to compete in the World Horseshoe Sandwich Eating Competition in Illinois, and their mother was enjoying living at home, back in Florida.

PART I:
THURSDAY, AUGUST 12TH, 2006

CHAPTER 1
SWEET DREAMS, 5:58 A.M.

Fluorescent lighting drenched the grocery store and the two men walking down aisle seven didn't appear to be shopping for anything in particular. Dustin, nearly six-foot-tall with dirty blonde hair, was wearing a red sweatshirt. Jack wore a blue jumper and stood to Dustin's left, near the center of the aisle. Jack's hair was short – the color of pumpkin pie. He gazed down the length of the aisle, transfixed on the vibrant tones of the two rainbow-colored walls of canned fruits and vegetables. No longer listening to Dustin's problems, Jack felt extremely relaxed. The brief moment of serenity evaporated as a familiar voice struck his hears, coming from an unfamiliar place – the store's intercom system. First, Jack looked around, baffled. Then he appeared to ask the ceiling its name, "Is that Bob Costas?"

"Say what, chief?" Queried Dustin.

"What...chief." Jack responded smugly, pausing for effect.

"Huh?"

After the confusion passed, Jack spoke first, "Um, I just heard Bob Costas describing us over the store's intercom system."

"You're crazy. Wait, did he describe you as a nerdy pre-pubescent?" Dustin heckled.

"No." Jack glared, but continued, "You didn't hear him?"

"This Robbie Williams classic has been playing since aisle five. By the way, how could you see me wearing this sweatshirt and decide to put that one on?" Dustin was perturbed. "Don't you have a sweater or a jacket, or a long-sleeved undershirt to keep you warm? Christ, Jack, we look like those goons from Double Dragon."

"Man, it's a grocery store. Nobody cares. I definitely thought I heard Costas make a storewide announcement about us, though. It sounded real."

"Jack, from what I know, Bob Costas is a straight shooter and if he didn't in some way describe you as scrawny, well, it might jeopardize his reputation. So, it probably wasn't him. Seriously, if you could control the crazy shit you say out loud, you could probably create a couple more opportunities for yourself in the real world, with normal girls."

"So…you didn't hear anything?"

"No. May I get back to my story, please? It's just that I kind of love Carrie, but her kid weirds me out. They didn't mean to have that kid and, I think it is safe to say that old Mario's death was not a loss for humanity. Do you think she'll let me put the little guy up for adoption?" Coming from anyone else, this question would have appalled Jack. However, such an insensitive comment was typical of Dustin. As Jack looked away, he noticed the canned food of aisle seven had transformed into bags of Doritos. He loved Doritos. Meanwhile, Dustin put a firm, brotherly hand on Jack's shoulder. Jack thought, *What happened to the peaches?* He snapped back into the moment when Dustin interrupted his thoughts.

"What in the world is wrong with you Jack? I know I ask you that all the time, but have you lost your mind? Your eyes are jumping all over the place. More importantly, you're not helping me solve my problem, here." Jack grabbed a shiny, blue bag of Cool Ranch Doritos, opened it, then spoke.

"Okay buddy, here's what I think. Haven't you noticed how bright it is in here? These lights are intense! You said that you "kind of love" Carrie. Do you realize you don't even respect her enough to stop getting other girls' phone numbers when we're out?" Jack paused and ate a single chip. Crunch! Then, he continued, "How do you expect her to react when you propose giving her only son, Mario Junior, up for adoption?"

Dustin had thought about this. He jumped in nodding his head eagerly as if he had a reasonable solution to the situation, "Honestly, I've thought about it. I could wine her and dine her before I pop the big question."

"May I stop you there?" Jack finished chewing, nibbled the cheese dust off the tips of his fingers, and began counting off his points. "We need to stop pretending, here. One, if you truly love her, you should think about modifying your behavior—which, I know, is difficult for you to understand. Two, these shelves were all canned food just a second ago. Now, they're bags of Doritos—which is a delicious alternative, but ultimately impossible. Three, Carrie and Mario never had a kid—and I'm positive that that Mario dude is still alive. Four, I certainly know the voice of Bob Costas when I hear it— he has narrated several of my dreams."

Dustin instantly became motionless. Jack stopped believing in him, and watched his friend disappear.

CHAPTER 2
WINGS, 6:23 A.M.

Jack jogged up and down the aisles of the store. His shoes squeaked on the waxed, linoleum floor like he was running wind sprints in a gymnasium. With each step he took, Jack felt more conscious—like his dream was solidifying. Even though he knew he was asleep, he was submerged in another reality. He thought about her dark hair— the long, uneven bangs that hung like soft, pointed, black icicles and clumped together in front of her cheeks when she looked down.

"Wings!" Jack shouted, trying to summon her. It didn't work and he felt pathetic.

When he came to the refrigerated section, he shivered from the rapid climate change. Frosted glass doorways led to the ice cream and frozen waffles. In the center of the aisle, there stood two forty-meter rows of waist-high coolers, filled with frozen pizza and vegetables. Jack became distracted by a bag of curly fries and lifted it from a cooler. He studied the label in detail: ten servings. The persuasiveness of his imagination astonished him while frosty bag stung his hand.

At that exact moment, a giant snowball burst through the roof and ceiling, and landed directly in the center of the aisle behind Jack. The violent crash, followed by a white poof startled him into an alarmed, protective stance. There was a dispersing ball of ice shards and dust in the air. The sunlight from the new hole in the ceiling shimmered off the particles like a spotlight cast on center stage. Wings appeared, covered in snow and lodged in between the carrots and the spinach. She wrapped her arms around her shoulders, shivering.

"Holy shit! Wings, are you okay?" Jack frightfully exclaimed. The young woman looked disoriented from her entrance, as Jack rushed over. He lifted Wings out of the cooler, and the snow fell off of her in clumps. The two sat on the floor, leaning against the metallic sides of the coolers. She shivered in his arms, and the wet chill transferred to his clothes.

"Jack, I got back as soon as I could! I didn't want to miss you." Then, she blurted out, "I want to become real!"

"Okay, *Pinocchio*, slow down," Jack said, sarcastically. "What do you mean?"

"What do I mean? What do *you* mean, *Pinocchio?* I'm serious. I'm done with this imaginary world. We've been meeting here for almost twenty years, now!"

"Well, not every night." Jack modified the statement. Wings' head turned sharply towards him, and her hair followed like soaked car-wash drapes.

"This is our opportunity, Mister Carpe Diem! You've had your whole life just how you wanted it, right? But you aren't happy, deep down. I can tell. How many times have you woken up alone, or after one of those drunken flings, knowing that you'll never see her again? You haven't been in a serious, meaningful relationship in years. I know you aren't looking for new adventures. You're just running away."

Jack was embarrassed, and he couldn't believe his own imagination was calling him out. Wings continued, "We've known each other for so long. Can't you admit to yourself that you really love me, and that's why you draw all those pictures? Even when you are awake, don't you wish I was there with you…in your bed with you?"

"Jesus! Okay, okay, yes, I do love you," Jack replied, "I would love for you to be real. Now, stop busting my stones." Jack, a so-called pragmatist, had just admitted he was in love with a figment of his imagination. In terms of self-respect, it was a low point.

On the other hand, Wings was exuberant. The last of the ice from her crash landing melted away and her skin rushed with color. The next night, she would be real again. She would get to have a real life, spent with her best friend, her lover, her future husband. She briefly thought of touching their real skin together. She bounced, and smiled with anticipation, kissed Jack on the face and mouth several times, like a woodpecker, and then pulled back.

"Let's fly somewhere!" She exclaimed. Jack nodded favorably. They started to float up through the hole in the ceiling. "It might be the last time we fly together, unless we're on an airplane," Wings giggled at the thought.

"You're crazy," Jack said.

"You're crazier," she replied.

The zinger amused young Chestnut. He was at peace with his psychosis. Wings lightheartedly flapped her arms, like always, as they ascended into the clouds. Jack laughed, then pulled her close.

"Anywhere in particular that you would like to go, dear?"

"Anywhere is paradise with you. Just take us somewhere different," Wings replied through the wind.

"Sounds good to me," Jack agreed. They were two hundred meters above the grocery store, which stood as a single building in an infinite rolling pasture. Wings twirled out of his arms, like a dancer, and the dream ended.

CHAPTER 3
LONDON TRAFFIC, 9:45 A.M.

Back in reality, it was Thursday morning when Jack opened his eyes. The red numbers on his clock radio told him it was 9:45. The sun burst through the window in perfect bands of light, revealing the clutter of garments on the floor. Jack's bedroom was a white, rectangular box with worn beige carpet and a modest balcony. There were three single beds, two dressers, and a mirror. His paintings and drawings covered the walls. Many of the pictures were of Wings, from different dreams. The urban morning noises were faint in the background. Wings was gone again; Jack was alone again; and everything seemed normal. He recognized reality immediately and wished he were still asleep.

As Jack got out of bed, he felt like he had no past at all. He lethargically stretched and farted to greet anonymity. It smelled dreadful. At breakfast, he ate Cheerios with his left hand and sketched the memory of Wings standing in the cooler at the grocery store with the other. He decided to go to the park and then the library after breakfast, dressed warmly, and left the apartment, somewhat surprised by the bright, mid-morning sun.

The empty sidewalk was typical for a weekday. The rows

of potted plants smelled like they were cooking in the sun, which reminded Jack of a farmer's market. He was listening to Phillip Glass' *Dance No. 8* through his headphones. Its unrelenting intensity against the motionless, clear skies above made him feel like he was in slow motion. The truth was that he was still pretty stoned, and not walking terribly fast to begin with. Nevertheless, he pushed ahead, watching his feet and not much else as he walked down the street.

Further down the block, at the corner of Chilworth and Gloucester, a caterpillar searched for a leaf on its tragically wayward journey up a lamppost. Erik headed north on Gloucester Terrace in his blue Fiat van. He was eager to get home and reheat last night's lasagna. Nancy, who liked technology, but often didn't know how to use it, was driving east on Chilworth Street. "It's a splendid BMW," Nancy said. She had one hand on the wheel and the other on her phone, neglecting the new car's hands-free features.

The most peculiar thing in view was Bones, a sizable vulture drifting on the wind high above the intersection. She was upset.

Nancy noticed the vulture first…rather, she observed as the vulture's fecal matter arrived on her windshield. The amount of bird shit obstructed her view, causing her to miss the traffic signal's change from green to red. *Oh fuck,* Jack and Erik thought, as the vehicles collided like some giant three-year-old had bashed them together. Erik's van had won. The crash launched broken glass and BMW pieces into the air above, around, and towards Jack, who stood frozen in shock a few short meters away.

Nancy's displaced tires squealed as they reluctantly dragged across the street until... Crack! The front left side of the white BMW firmly struck the lamppost that stood between Jack and the street. A small plate on the lamppost burst off the base, then flew past Jack, cutting him across his left calf. He winced as he studied the rest of the post. The lamp moaned in metallic agony as its top-heavy structure gave way to gravity, then crashed to the ground at

Jack's feet.

It was over. A line of blood dripped down his leg and off the edge of his sneaker. "Holy shit," Jack said, exasperated, and grasped his leg where the flying piece of lamppost had sliced it, as a small puddle of red grew beneath the sole of his shoe.

Erik was unharmed in the accident and was the first to react. He got out of his van and dialed 112. Nancy pulled her frazzled head off the airbag and looked around. She had lost her cell phone in the debris. Bones suspended herself discreetly in the breeze above the chaos, looking for signs of a feast. There were no dead bodies, but Jack was bleeding. This caught her attention.

CHAPTER 4
HYDE PARK, 12:30 P.M.

It was hard to determine the exact moment that the wind changed from calm to breezy...it just happened. Jack watched the invisible hand catch the smoke from his cigarette and drag it away. The constable at the scene finished writing his report and handed it to Jack to sign. Distracted by the thought of flying a kite, he signed the statement, finally able to continue his walk south. Behind him, at the intersection of Gloucester and Chilworth, there was a mix of workers methodically erasing the evidence of the crash.

Three blocks later, Jack approached a shop with a sign that read, Dalton & Nelson: Stationary, Gifts, and More. He stopped and went inside. In the back of the store, he found a thin, arched plastic kite with streamers featuring a cartoon picture of a dolphin and a purple octopus playing in the sea. It was the most conservative of the £2 kites. He purchased the kite, walked across the street, and entered Hyde Park with it sticking out of his bag.

He started the afternoon reclined against a tree. His pants had a small tear, but the emergency response team gave him a bandage for the cut on his leg. He was oblivious to the escaped vulture that had followed him and perched on the tree above. Jack removed *The Old Man and the Sea* from his bag, undid his blue, rubber band bookmark, and read.

Several meters away, an attractive, young woman wearing green corduroy jeans watched her son play with a plastic rake. Jack noted it as the most boring toy he'd ever seen. After Jack had finished the novella, it was time to get busy. He un-wrapped the kite, quickly assembled it, and a gust of wind lifted it away with ease. The whole process took only a few minutes.

The tug of the kite reminded Jack of fishing. Lost in the moment, he imagined the ocean. Jack was proud of his spontaneity. Routines can be important, but they can also make you boring. Jack's fear was that he would end up doing the same thing for so long that he couldn't remember one year from another. In fact, he liked to do something interesting or potentially life-altering almost every day, just to keep a mental diary. You could call him a performance artist, but that would be giving him too much credit.

This kite was a great idea, Chestnut thought, with a big smile on his face as it tugged at his arm like a puppy. *Too big a smile, maybe? I probably look like a pedophile.* Immediately, he replaced his expression with a resting glare. He lit a cigarette and looked around, intentionally ignoring the kite pulling at his wrist. He looked at his watch, which his brother had given him for his birthday. The battery was dead—the hands laid motionless at five o'clock. He glanced back and forth for several minutes while he smoked, and nobody seemed to notice. Jack felt lonely.

Emily had broken Jack's heart—of that, there was no question. People said that due to the trauma of the event, he'd suffered a nervous breakdown, from which he never truly recovered. This final emotional blow had broken his cracked psychological piñata.

Jack watched the kite and listened to the wind. It distracted him from his life. He forgot about the car accident, the loss of his father and sister, his old friends, and the calm air before the breeze came. He lived in the moment, and for an instant, he thought about letting his kite go—just to see it swim away in the wind. At that moment, Bones leapt from the tree and took flight.

CHAPTER 5
VULTURES, 3:46 P.M.

The sun struck the bird from the west and announced her presence with a long shadow that crawled across the ground. Jack was looking up when his stomach spiraled south in unison with the bird. The vulture flew past his kite and turned on the wind. It became evident to Jack that it was no longer simply riding the currents. The bird circled him twice, then flew off.

Jack looked around, wondering who else had just seen the giant bird. A couple laughed while walking on the path. "Green Jeans" watched her son. A jogger with headphones and red shorts ran by, followed shortly by a man in a suit walking his dog and talking on a cell phone. No one saw the vulture, so Jack carried on as if the bird were never there.

Less than five minutes later, Green Jeans' son was pointing at Jack's kite. Jack made eye contact with Ms. Jeans, and they shared a flummoxed smile before her face contorted with a sort of parental terror.

"Kyle!" She yelled and stood up. Kyle was rumbling towards Jack and his kite— anxiously thrusting out his tiny hands. Jack looked to Kyle's mother for official approval. She nodded affirmatively as she approached, and Jack passed little Kyle the string. The child grabbed it eagerly and the kite jerked in his hands. He giggled. Green Jeans laughed too. When she was close enough for Jack to introduce himself, he opened his mouth and Kyle let go of his kite. Suddenly, instead of getting this woman's name, Jack was watching Mother Nature escort his brand-new kite fifty meters downwind in a jagged, horizontal *whoosh*. Jack's mouth hung low. "Kyle!" Green Jeans shrieked with embarrassment.

The kite gradually shrank into the distance, then disappeared behind some trees. After the shared moment of astonishment had passed, Green Jeans yelled at her son. Jack—feeling the opportunity had slipped away, having no kite to fly, and feeling uncomfortable—decided it was time to walk to the library.

He said an awkward goodbye, then left the park and headed towards Paddington Square.

Five minutes later, the bird flew over Jack again, but he didn't notice when their shadows crossed. He walked on, oblivious, as the shadow of Bones dipped and raced across the street, people, and cars next to him. She finally perched on the corner of a bank, which overlooked the Westminster Library. The late afternoon breeze carried grey-bottomed clouds that whispered rain to her instincts. The vulture was hungry but didn't have the energy to keep searching for food, so she decided to wait a bit longer to see if Jack was going to die.

CHAPTER 6
A BLESSING AND A CURSE, 5:27 P.M.

The door to the Westminster Library was old and cumbersome. It reminded Jack of the lid of a treasure chest. This was a rather appropriate metaphor because the resources of the library are entertainment gold for the underprivileged and desperate. They have free books, CDs, movies, even internet—which is a big deal when you can't afford any of these things. After returning the copy of *The Old Man and the Sea* that he had borrowed, Jack used one of the computers to search the web.

He checked his bank accounts. He was still poor but, despite that fact, he couldn't wait to move to Greece. His plan was to get drunk and sleep outside in a hammock for a whole month. He wanted to set the record for consecutive hours in a hammock, but then he realized he'd eventually have to use the bathroom. He'd have to settle for the record of the drunkest man in a hammock.

After using the computer, he noticed a cute girl with chocolate-colored hair and a yellow t-shirt reading the newspaper, downstairs by the philosophy and periodical section. Jack strolled over to get a good look at her, but then felt extremely creepy when she looked up from her newspaper and directly into his eyes. Suddenly self-aware and embarrassed, Jack picked up a random book, entitled *The Book of the Die*. He flipped towards the center and began to read.

"A man who asks, 'What is the meaning of life?', and means it, is either very young or very boring. In a youngster, the question can be forgiven since all he really means is, 'Why can't I get laid?', but in an oldster, one whose prick has been stroked a few times by someone besides himself, the question is an embarrassment." Jack nodded. He sat down and continued reading intently while the brunette finished her article, got up, and left.

Outside, Bones the vulture remained perched on the roof across the street from the library. Jack exited the building, and the raptor stretched her wings. Unaware of her presence, he cursed to himself, staring at the rain clouds. The strap of his messenger bag dug hard into his shoulder with the weight of the books and CDs he had borrowed from the library. He was hungry. It was 5:30 and Queensway bustled with people coming home from work. A rainstorm was inevitable. Jack didn't have an umbrella but speculated that it would take him fifteen minutes to get home—and with a little bit of luck, he'd beat the rain.

The first cold drop of water landed on Jack's arm with a *plop*, foiling his plan. It beaded into smaller droplets and covered his skin in goose bumps. Jack walked south towards the Kentucky Fried Chicken (KFC) across from Whiteley's. He whistled George Michael's *Careless Whispers* while passing among the people. Bones stalked, overhead. She was flying in figure eights, disappearing and then re-appearing from behind the buildings.

Jack watched as a jagged lightning bolt stretched across and illuminated the overcast sky. The reverberating thunderclap helped shake the water from the clouds, like a dog shaking water from its fur. Umbrellas burst into the air sporadically, like multicolored nylon popcorn, as the stampeding sound of raindrops came from the west. People without umbrellas skirted to nearby overhangs for shelter. Jack, confident in his bag's waterproof lining, continued walking as if it weren't even raining. He smiled to himself and whistled *Singin' in the Rain* as his shoes began to squish and squash on the pavement.

The bell rang as Jack opened the glass door of KFC. It smelled like fried chicken, exactly as he expected, and he was the only customer. He immediately felt the chilly air working its way through his wet clothes. He ordered one bucket of chicken—all drumsticks. It seemed like a relatively insignificant request. However, he received a distressed look from the young gentleman who took the order. While he waited, Jack twisted out his thoroughly soaked wristband over the trash can. Four minutes, twelve chicken legs, and £15 later, he bent and crammed the greasy, paper bucket into his bag.

Back on the street, Jack had a strange feeling as he approached his apartment. He looked up, but falling water landed in his eyes and he felt stupid for staring into the rain. He walked south, turned left, and continued east. The cold wind gave him a soggy push, and he looked forward to being home.

Ten minutes later, Jack took a heavy step out of the elevator and stood in the hallway. He knew Bridget was home when he heard the club music booming outside the flat. Jack opened the door, and some unpleasant beats escaped into the hall. The lamp and kitchen light were on. Bridget was on the phone, talking over the music as if there were a DJ in the flat and she had no control over the volume. The rain and twilight glowed in the main windows behind her. She draped her smooth, athletic legs over the chair's arm. She paired a thin cotton shirt with the tiny blue and pink shorts that crinkled in the creases of her thighs. She immediately gave Jack a look that said, *"Oh my god, mate! You're so soaking wet!"* Even Bridget's body language had an Australian accent. She talked on the phone while Jack walked into the kitchen to unload.

Jack often wondered how one person could be so sexy and so annoying at the same time. Bridget was like a Ferrari with a broken, blaring car horn, which made her hard to appreciate. For Jack, talking with her was as rewarding as having a conversation with a television set.

"I know!" Bridget shouted into the phone, "My flat mate just got home, and he's soaked! Alright, mate. Then we're sorted. Nine o'clock. Don't forget the drugs." She laughed into the receiver, then repeated, "Drugs, drugs, drugs," then giggled again to herself.

She repeated everything, just to hear herself say it in different ways: spinach, balloons, sort it out. The meaning or usage of the echoed word was irrelevant. Jack walked over and turned down the radio volume so they could talk. Bridget frowned at him as she hung up the phone.

"Don't you think," Jack said evenly, "that it's a little ridiculous to yell over your own music while you're on the phone?"

"Don't lecture me on ridiculous," Bridget shouted, "You're the one who is soaking wet. You just don't like my music!"

"First, my degree of wetness is an entirely different sort of ridiculous; and second, it's true, your taste in music is awful, but I actually turned it down so we wouldn't have to shout!"

"Sort it out, man!"

Not feeling like arguing, Jack quickly changed the subject by asking, "How was work?"

Bridget forgot they were yelling, "Great! I cut an attorney's hair today. He was gorgeous! He tipped me fifty quid! Then, he asked for my phone number. Then, I was on the train and this gross bum kept staring at me, but I just kept thinking about the egg salad sandwich I had for lunch. It was so good. And I noticed a stain on my dress. It was so silly. I'm going out on a date tonight with this guy, Kevin. He's really cute. I work with him on Tuesdays. I think we're going to Thrillers…"

Jack continued to unpack his things while Bridget kept talking about her day. This was a common occurrence. Jack put the bucket of chicken on the kitchen counter and placed his library books and CDs in his room. He removed his wet clothes and hung them over the railing of the narrow balcony outside. He changed the bandage on his leg, then put on a clean, warm pair of jeans and a t-shirt.

"How was your day?" Bridget shouted from the living room. Jack came out of his room.

"What?" He yelled. Bridget held up Jack's sketch pad and the picture of Wings from the grocery store.

"Oh, I love her hair! I'm totally going to cut someone's hair like that," she said.

"Cool. Is that what you said, before?"

"Before, I said, 'How was your day?' Tell me about it. I want to know!"

"Oh. Okay, it was pretty crazy, actually," Jack began, "I was on my way to the park this afternoon, and there was this car accident right in…"

"Oh my God!" Bridget interrupted, "I just remembered this car crash from a couple months ago…" She proceeded to tell a story about a car accident she had seen, and how she started talking to the cop afterward, and he asked for her phone number because she was a witness. She gave Jack a wink, completely forgetting she had asked him anything at all.

Most times, Jack didn't even bother wasting his energy on conversation with his roommate. Whatever instinctual satisfaction there was in telling a story to someone, Bridget sucked that urge out of Jack like a vacuum. He decided to save his story. Bridget kept talking.

"I'm not sure what to wear on this date. Does this red dress make me look like a tart?" Jack gave her a subtle, accusing glare but said nothing. "Sort it out, man!" She shouted. To make peace, Jack shook the crumpled bucket of KFC and asked,

"Would you like some?"

"KFC? Sure! I'll take a wing."

"There are only drumsticks."

"That's stupid. Why?"

"It's my favorite piece."

"What if someone else wanted a different piece?" Bridget pretended to be concerned. Jack, aggravated by her again, replied, "Do you want a piece, or not?"

"I'd like a wing."

"You're such a pain in the ass."

This statement satisfied Bridget. She smiled and walked over to grab a drumstick from the bucket, then drew back quickly.

"There are, like, legs from ten different chickens in there!"

"Twelve maybe, depending on how deformed they were. Maybe they're all lefts."

"Gross," she said, as she apprehensively picked a piece out of the bucket.

"Gorgeous," Jack contradicted, when he remembered something he wanted to ask her, awkwardly blurting out, "I need a haircut."

"Have you been buttering me up or something?" Bridget asked, and then took a bite of chicken.

Buttering her up? I didn't even think I was being nice. Jack watched her chew for a moment. "No, no, no! It's just," he paused, "you're like a cross between Paul Mitchell and Jessica Alba."

"Oh, shut up! I do not look like Jessica Alba! You're teasing me." Bridget laughed and blushed, "How about Sunday?"

"Sunday!" Jack whined. Bridget stopped blushing. The moment was lost.

"Mate, that is the soonest! I'm going out of town this weekend, to a festival in Manchester. You don't even need one."

Bridget sauntered to the bathroom to put on her makeup and talked the whole time about the Chester Fest. Jack grabbed his book from his room and sat down on the couch. Bridget finished applying her makeup, but Jack couldn't tell the difference.

About thirty minutes later, there was a knock on the door. Jack answered it.

Kevin was a tall, skinny, Australian guy with a dyed-blonde mohawk, sporting black pants and a leather jacket. Jack had expected someone more attractive. Bridget was not yet ready, so Jack offered Kevin a drumstick out of hospitality. Fortunately for Jack, he declined. To avoid small talk, Jack continued reading. Kevin fidgeted with a buckle on his jacket while he waited. When Bridget was finally ready, she came out of her room in a black skirt and red sweater, with an umbrella in her left hand.

Soon after they left, Jack pulled a rubber band from his wrist and wrapped it around the spine of his novel as a make-shift bookmark. He turned on the television and flipped through some channels until he settled on the second half of *American Ninja* ('85), starring Michael Dudikoff, on BBC Three. Fifteen minutes later, he was asleep on the couch.

CHAPTER 7
GHOST STORY, 11:14 P.M.

On screen, a campfire's light streaks a patch of orange into the brisk, October dusk. The six campers: Dan, Irene, Ted, Shelly, Marion, and Jordan, sit on colorful blankets in a semicircle around the burning stack of off-cuts of wood and branches.

The camera pans across the individuals. First, is Dan. He sits by himself, playing with a large flashlight. His legs, atrophied from progressive arthritis, are a topic of gossip and laughter behind his back. Irene, a plus-sized Filipino, sits next to a much skinnier girl, named Marion. Together, they talk about Leslie, another teenager from school. Standing in a leather bomber jacket, twisting his long, thin mustache, with his shifty eyes constantly glaring at whoever is talking, is Ted. Next to him is his new girlfriend, Shelly. She is trying to discuss her favorite movies with Jordan, but he's only half-listening—he is mostly trying to hear what Irene is saying about Leslie.

Dan turns the flashlight under his chin. He slants his eyebrows up and down, unsure which has the scariest effect. He slowly turns his head to look at everyone, and then rubs his hands together on the flashlight, ghoulishly asking,

"Does anybody want to hear a ghost story?"

Irene's, Shelly's, and Marion's eyes all light with excitement, while Ted's roll unfavorably to the dark sky above. Then, Ted says, still looking up, "Isn't telling a ghost story creepy enough with those brittle, deformed legs of yours? Do you really need the upside-down flashlight gimmick? Besides, I'm pretty sure this story's gonna blow." Everyone else tries to un-hear Ted's thoughtless and hurtful remarks, encouraging Dan to begin his story.

"It was a night much like this one," Dan pauses for effect.

"Cliché," Ted coughs.

"Somewhere on this very mountain, mean, old Arden Fowler stood over a cutting board, alone in his cabin where he prepared his favorite meal: Manwich!—with real bits of men. Fowler was a schizophrenic-turned-mountain cannibal. He was thus, insane, and his exploits were so gruesome that police often misattributed them to the acts of starving bears. It was his misplaced notoriety that made Fowler take things to the next level.

""I killed those people!" The cannibal lifted the cleaver, listening to the news on the radio. Chop! "Not bears!" Chop! "I am the bear!" Chop! He tilted the cutting board and slid the cut-up bits of a human arm into the simmering, seasoned broth. That was when Fowler had his blackest epiphany."

"Where's the fucking pussy, gimp?" Ted interrupts.

"Oh, my God! Ted, you're such a pig!" Marion shouts, upset that Ted has interrupted Dan's horrific tale. "Go on, Dan. The story's great, so far!"

Ted slaps Shelly's arm, and she winces. Knowing what he wants, Shelly grabs an orange pill bottle out of her purse, removes a few tablets, and hands them to Ted. He tosses them into his mouth and chases them down with the rest of his beer, then throws the empty beer can on Marion's blanket. Dan's story is on hold.

"Asshole!" Jordan yells.

"Shut up, bitch!" Ted shouts back.

"Just ignore him," Marion says. There is an uncomfortable pause, but Dan continues,

"Umm… well, Fowler was driving to loony town in a car with no breaks. The equipment he needed wasn't cheap, but he got it. The kidnapping of the brain surgeon, Doctor Russell, was easy, compared to the hunting, tranquilizing, and wheelbarrowing of the grizzly bear from the woods into his cabin—his diabolical operation was finally ready."

Ted interjects, again. This time, with a long, *Buuuurrrrp!* Dan pauses in frustration, but continues, nonetheless.

"Torture, killing, and cannibalism weren't enough for Fowler. His hunger for dominance was the most extreme. He wanted power and size beyond that of a human. He wanted terrible claws and fierce teeth. Terror in the eyes of his victims was his drug of choice, and he knew exactly how he was going to up the dose. Arden Fowler was going to put his brain into the body of a bear!"

"Holy fucking gay!" Ted shouts, now standing in front of the beer cooler. "This piece of shit just hit the fucking mountain. This story is awful!" Ted digs into his pocket and pulls out a folded sheet of wax paper filled with cocaine. He swiftly inhales it, then rubs his nose. He licks his hand, then cracks open another free Miller Lite™. Ted's bravado appalls the entire group. They sit, staring at him in collective silence. "I'm not sorry! You can finish your garbage story if you want."

Dan looks at Marion and continues, "What happened that night was unspeakable. The talented Doctor Russell had surgically brought a curse into the world. He believed that if he did what Fowler asked of him, he'd be set free, but there was no mercy granted. Never trust a cannibal." Dan's audience nods in agreement. "Just as the sunlight struck the morning fog, an unholy monster came forth from the cabin. In the coming weeks, the startling rise in bear attacks finally led to a full investigation. When the police unfolded the truth, it was too late. Inside Fowler's den, everything was painted red with dried blood. Chairs, backpacks, scalpels, and shoes were all covered in a nightmarish, crimson Pollock motif. There was no Doctor Russell, no Arden Fowler, no bear—just a big note clawed into the wall that read…" Dan leaned forward, "King Klaws is coming, and you can kiss my bear ass!" Dan finishes the story by shining the flashlight down on his partially exposed butt cheek. Marion, Jordan, Irene, and Shelly gasp. They love Dan's thrilling story.

"I was really scared," Irene says, with her hand pressed against her chest.

"I was scared of Dan's ass!" Jordan announces, with his prominent lisp. Shelly and Dan laugh, too.

"You're mean," Marion responds, giving Dan a coy smile. He smiles back.

"That story fucking sucked!" Ted exclaims, before tilting his sixteen-ounce beer above his head. "It wasn't even a ghost story! That was a brain transplant story, beef jerky legs. I've had scarier nachos."

"Stop being a bully!" Irene argues.

Ted points at her and replies, "Tell it to Jenny Craig." He swigs his beer and then turns his attention to Dan. "Dan, seriously, first, where was the pussy? Where was the passion?" Ted humps the air for a moment.

"Gross!" Irene cries. Ted spits beer towards her, then pretends to throw the can at Jordan, who flinches. Ted laughs and throws the empty can into the woods.

"Cool it down!" Jordan says, his feminine side flaring.

"Cool it down?" Ted says, mocking Jordan's voice. "You're lucky I don't whoop the shit out of you, Tinkerbelle." Ted turns to Shelly, "You know how much I fucking can't stand homos."

Dan, like a badger about to attack, clenches his jaw tight. His cheeks twitch in anticipation of a fight. His legs don't have enough muscle to support his fragile body. *If only I could walk!* He thinks.

"What's that, Tiny Tim? I know you don't have the balls

to say something to me," Ted continues, reading Dan's mind. "You're a helpless cripple! Guess what? You say one word I don't like and I'm going to humiliate you like I did last New Year's."

Dan remembers how embarrassing that could be, glancing over at Marion. Ted senses Dan's feelings for her like a sarcastic Darth Vader. In a softened voice, Ted adds, "What? You're afraid of looking like a helpless bitch in front of Marion?" He pauses, looking around for a reaction from his captive audience. "News flash! You are a helpless bitch. And Marion? She's as shallow as a fucking kiddy pool," Ted laughs, amused with himself. "You and I know old two-fingers-in-the-throat Parker is never gonna have sex with you! Your legs look like petrified twigs. You're a freak. It would kill her rep. I mean, she'd be known as the girl that had sex with Danny Pretzel Legs. And what the fuck are you looking at, Irene? You want some of this? I'd tell you to start throwing up like Marion does, you pork chop, but even if you did puke off thirty-five pounds, you'd still look like a fucking goblin from Lord of the Rings.

"Wait, Dan. I'm not done with you. It's not like you're out playing sports after school. It's not like you're juggling girlfriends, like me." Shelly gives Ted a disapproving frown. He continues, "Maybe you could use that free time to make up a better story—something with some fervor!" Ted shakes his head in disappointment, "I need a smoke." Shelly starts to get up too, but Ted stops her, "No, you stay here. Your voice annoys me. I'll come back and get some head later, before I go to sleep." Shelly's eyes begin to well with tears.

Ted grabs a beer for the walk. "And next time, Dan, buy some real beer." Ted takes one last look at their shocked faces, "What? Fuck you. I'm not sorry." He turns and marches towards the pond. His footsteps grow fainter as he walks deeper into the woods. When the group is sure he's gone, Dan speaks.

"I didn't make up that story."

"Let's play some music," Marion suggests.
"Great idea!".

CHAPTER 8
BRIDGET, 11:15 P.M.

The light from the movie projector reflected onto the screen and back into the eyes of the fifty people watching the opening credits of the late-90's cult classic, *King Klaws*. It was famous for its gritty writing and direction by James Repici, and a breakthrough performance by a young actor, named Dustin Switch, who played the infamous Ted Baldwin.

Bridget and Kevin were a few minutes into the movie, late Thursday night, in Theater Three of the British multi-club, Thrillers. They sat in the middle seats, near the front row.

"Oh, my God!" Bridget yelled, and turned to Kevin, "I totally know that bloke." *Is she trying to talk over the movie? I'm right here*, Kevin thought. He whispered back,

"Which one?"

"The guy with that long, curly mustache," Bridget said, possibly louder than before.

"Ted?" he asked.

"No, no mate. His name is Dustin."

"Oh, well maybe, yeah? But in the movie, his character's name is Ted."

"Mate, sort it out! He's the only guy on the bloody screen

with a mustache. I don't know his movie name. I've just met him before. He's an actor."

A resounding *Shhhh!* came from several rows back. Bridget shoved a middle finger above her seat in the general direction of the request for silence. *Hell! Is she hard-of-hearing? Kevin thought. They just said his name in the bloody movie and she's over here shouting like a nutter.* He stared at Bridget, then at the film, and once again at her in disbelief, then put his arm around her shoulder. She lowered her arm, and they continued watching the film.

In the movie, Dan told the story of Arden Fowler, and Ted/Dustin kept interrupting him.

Bridget watched Dustin acting on the big screen—he looked so young. It was exciting. She couldn't help but daydream about the last time they had sex. She remembered holding the kitchen faucet in the apartment as their thrusts kept pushing her stomach against the cold, black marble countertop. His right hand was firmly holding her hip bone and his left hand…

"So how do you know him?" Kevin whispered.

"Who?"

"The guy with the mustache!"

"Oh, he's my flat mate's best friend. He comes over to the apartment, now and then."

"Does he always have that stupid thing on his face?"

"No. Actually, I've never seen him with a mustache. I think it's pretty hot!"

"Are you taken' the piss? He looks like Dick-fucking-Dastardly! Do you like that goofy yank, or something?"

"Yeah, he's my right boyfriend. I shag him all the time. Come on now! I don't even know the guy!"

Shhhh!

Bridget pretended to watch the movie to avoid further interrogation. Kevin removed his hand from the back of her chair.

In the movie, Dan finishes his story about the legend of King Klaws. Ted continues his ridicule and intimidation of

Dan and the other campers. The audience, as usual, began to respond to his vicious and offensive monologue by yelling at his character in the movie. First, someone shouted, "You're a right tosser, Ted!" A couple of people laughed. Boos, laughter, and people throwing popcorn and insults towards the screen accompanied everything Ted did or said after that. Bridget wasn't having fun anymore. Kevin was acting like a jerk, and everyone was so mean to Dustin's character. Bridget reminded herself that it was just a movie, and they didn't know the real Dustin.

In the film, Ted stands at the edge of Hick's Pond in the moonlight. He chugs the last of his beer, finishes his cigarette, and tosses them both into the water.

Someone in the audience shouted, "You're killing the planet, asshole!"

Ted unzips his pants and urinates at the water's edge. Staggering from the alcohol and drugs, he walks around, even though he hasn't stopped pissing yet. Dark piano music begins to play.

Theater Three grew silent. In the stillness of the moment, the bass music could be heard and felt coming from Club One.

CHAPTER 9
THRILLERS, 11:39 P.M.

Originally, Thrillers was a movie theater with three auditoriums, a refreshment lobby, and a marquee over the entrance. In 1998, a group of investors bought the property and converted it into a mega-club. Thanks to some well-placed marketing, it became an overnight success. The new owners subdivided the auditoriums into Club One, Bar Two, and Theater Three. The £5 cover included entrance to all three venues and free popcorn from the lobby—which was an event location in and of itself.

Club One played electronic dance music and hip-hop. The split-level, glass dance floor was the centerpiece of Thrillers' investments. Club One incorporated the auditorium's surround sound with lights and smoke. Behind the dance floors, a thirty-by-seventy-foot movie screen played video footage taken by a jet flying through clouds on a sunny day.

Bar Two was more relaxed than the other floors, with a large selection of beer, whiskey, and live music. There was a long, old bar down the right-side wall, and pool tables and dart boards down the left side. The owners had removed all but the back few rows of seats and constructed a stage in front of the screen for live performances.

Theater Three, the smallest auditorium, remained in its original condition. It played cult classics and posted its schedule and show times on the Thrillers website. Theater Three in particular, had a rather dubious reputation for sex, sex sales, drug use, drug sales, and drunken people passing out, left undiscovered until the lights came on at sunrise.

CHAPTER 10
VICTIMOLOGY, 11:40 P.M.

On the screen, the doomed campers sing along to the chorus of Don McLean's iconic *American Pie*, "Singing this will be the day that I die! This will be the day that I die." Shelly smiles anxiously as she peers into the dark woods.

In the theater, Bridget could tell that the ecstasy she and Kevin had taken had hit her blood streams, as her skin became hot and tingly. "Do you feel anything?" Bridget said, boldly piercing the quiet of the auditorium.

"Babe, could you please try to whisper? Yeah, I'm starting to feel it a little bit."

Bridget could tell Kevin was perturbed about something. His acting bothered upset her, in turn. Suddenly, she couldn't stop thinking about sex. She grabbed his left arm and rubbed it firmly.

Back on the screen, the not-so-loveable Ted Baldwin steps on a bear trap. It flings shut a couple of inches below his knee, breaking his leg like a matchstick. He howls in agony.

In the auditorium, Bridget and some of the audience screamed, but the majority cheered. She clenched onto Kevin's arm and he inched closer to her in turn.

Ted is reeling in pain. He squirms in the iron grip of the

trap, doing everything in his drunken might to pry it open. Then comes the sound of giant footsteps: *Thump! Thump!* and the cracks of breaking underbrush, *Thump!* Ted stares into the shadows. The bear's foot emerges from the darkness and plants firmly into the ground several yards in front of where Ted is ensnared.

Nine-foot-tall, weighing two thousand pounds, the humongous, expressionless grizzly bear stands wearing a park ranger's hat. "Holy shit! It's Smokey the Bear! I'm fucking saved!" Ted rejoices. The bear begins a deep, rolling, sardonic laugh. Ted's expression turns to bewilderment. "What's so funny, Smokey?" He naïvely states.

The bear laughs even harder, until it begins to cough like an old smoker, then falls on all fours and starts a cat-like convulsion. When the bear's cute hat falls off, it reveals a ring of stitches around his skull that resembles a miniature train track at the base of a Christmas tree.

The bear coughs a few more times before *Hauwck!* A shredded, blood-soaked park ranger uniform shoots from King Klaws' mouth and lands on the dirt in front of Ted.

Oh no, that's not Smokey the Bear, Bridget thought, holding Kevin's arm tighter.

The bear stands up again, blood and saliva dripping from the points of his sharp, menacing teeth. He darts towards Ted and stands up, about to strike.

"Wait! Hold on!" Ted screams. The bear pauses. "I have friends." Ted continues, "I can lure them over here. Shit, we can eat them together! Deal?" The bear abruptly grabs Ted's arm and effortlessly snatches it from his body at the shoulder. He holds it by the wrist and strips the flesh from the bone. Ted screams in pain and horror.

"Yum," King Klaws grunts, in a deep, growling bear voice.

"I hope you fucking choke!" Ted cries, indignantly. In response to this, the bear forces his pointer claw in little Teddy's mouth, then jerks down, ripping off the lower half of his face.

Blood, teeth, and jaw land on the dirt next to the trap. Ted lets out a gargled, unintelligible scream as his tongue dangles in the night air. The bear then places his giant, sharp pointer against Ted's bloody neck below his Adam's apple, then thrusts the tip of his claw down into the top of Ted's chest. Blood spurts out of the wound. Using this approach, the bear holds Ted's mutilated body in place. Then, grabs his head with his free paw. To finish the process, King Klaws rips backward, separating Teddy's head and spine from his ribs and torso. His insides fall out his newly created orifice. The blood-spattered bear grins, staring at the camera, and enthusiastically resounds, "Ribs are my favorite."

The crowd responded in a chorus of laughter and disgust. *Poor Dustin*, Bridget thought, then nuzzled her head into Kevin's shoulder.

Next, the movie cuts back to Irene, who is eating a pork rib from a Tupperware container while Shelly expresses concern for her "Teddy Bear," before ultimately heading off into the woods to find him.

Back in the theater, Kevin was no longer upset at Bridget's lack of movie etiquette. He had come there because he thought it would lead to him getting laid, so he decided to start worrying about that. The weight of Bridget's head sunk into his shoulder. He leaned over and tried to kiss her on the mouth, but she turned away.

"What?" Kevin asked. Bridget slowly got out of her seat and slid into his lap like an erotic dancer. She faced him and not the screen, then pushed her chest up against his and leaned into his neck while grinding her pelvis into him. She whispered in his ear,

"Does this feel good?"

Fuck, I knew she could whisper, Kevin grinned.

"Sit down, you stupid bitch!" A burly-sounding voice stated from the darkness behind them. Kevin gave Bridget a concerned look, not taking the opportunity to speak in her defense.

She was not impressed—in fact, she was not pleased with the whole situation. Kevin had just lost his chance, but Bridget was still extremely horny, and she had other options. She got off of him, and back into her seat.

"Let's go dance," Bridget said, more annoyed than eager. Her cell phone buzzed in her purse from a new text message. She glanced at it as they left the theater, then smiled. It was from Dustin.

PART II:
FRIDAY, AUGUST 13TH, 2006

CHAPTER 11
THE NEXT DAY, 12:34 A.M.

As he walked towards work, Jack's dingy, black leather business shoes were tight and warm on his feet. The wooden front door of The Cask & Glass was about fifty meters in front of him. He felt tired, but didn't want to be late, so he marched a little faster.

The Cask & Glass was a three-story, red brick public house on the corner of Palace and Wilfred Street—a block north of Buckingham Palace. The pub, itself, occupied only the first floor. The second and third floors were where the manager, Mike Walsh, and his family lived. Outside of the pub sat white, metal tables and chairs, and potted flowers.

Wood-paneled walls with framed, black and white pictures lined the tiny interior. Fittingly, it made Jack feel like a bartender in someone's living room. The patrons, if they weren't engaged in conversation, faced the bar or watched the horse race on the small TV mounted in the upper left corner of the pub—these distractions allowed

Jack to enter undetected. He hung up his bag in the back room that connected the bar and the parlor. Then, he clocked-in, put on a black apron, grabbed a rag and his register key, washed his hands, and began his shift. It was 5:00.

At work, he felt like an authentic cog in British society. It was his second time working at this pub, after all. The regulars—a gang of middle-aged British alcoholics—were all present. Jack gave a customary smile as he entered the bar from the back room. Scott "Curly" Nickels, who had short, curly hair and round glasses, waited anxiously for the end of the shift change. He was leaning against the bar with a £50 note in hand. Jack started work by taking his order.

A round of drinks usually incorporated ninety percent of the customers in the pub and after that one order, Jack essentially had nothing to do but a couple of chores for twenty minutes, while he waited for the next round.

"A small bottle of Holsten for Bruce," Curly said with a wink (because bottles only came in one size). "Mary?" asked Curly.

"I'll have a chardonnay, darling!" Mary Singer spoke, her snout high in the air. Keith "Hampo" Hampton and Andrew entered the pub laughing and smiling. Then, like moths, they immediately turned their focus to the light emanating from the small television, which Bruce was already watching intently, remote in hand. Bruce un-muted the TV and everyone stopped what they were doing.

"Now, it's My Russian Princess making a move! My Russian Princess takes the inside on turn four! By a length! By two-lengths…"

"Struth! Look at that horse move!" Hampo exclaimed, putting a hand on Bruce's big shoulder.

"Yeah, sure." Bruce replied in a husky voice, under his breath, "She's galloping away with my bloody fifty quid." Hampo and Andrew chuckled, followed by Bruce, who couldn't help but laugh at himself. Hampo pensively looked at his watch—he was often late for dinner.

Meanwhile, Curly ordered Andrew and Hampo both a

pint of Spitfire Ale. The district attorney, Martin Sags, sat by the window, reading a newspaper and drinking a glass of scotch. Two gin and tonics sat in front of Mr. Novak and his wife, Mallory. He was dressed in his usual Mr. Monopoly fashion. She had a similar formal ensemble—reminiscent of an elderly Bride of Frankenstein. Mr. Novak tipped the brim of his top hat to Curly after Scott signaled that he was buying them drinks as well. Then, Scott ordered a vodka tonic for himself and a half-pint for Jack.

Jack punched the order into the register then read the total aloud, "£24.50."

"£24.50!" Curly replied, then rubbed his forehead and repeated the total a third time, "£24.50, is that it?" he added, jovially. He looked around with a big smile, his cheeks lifting up his glasses, then handed Jack the £50 note. Jack was already preparing the drinks, but paused, took the bill, and made the change. Behind Curley, it seemed extremely sunny outside, and strangely, Mike had not come downstairs to say hello, but Jack didn't dwell on it. He finished preparing and serving the gang their beverages, then grabbed a dustpan and broom from the back to sweep the outside area—one of his few side jobs.

CHAPTER 12
THINGS GOT WEIRD, 12:40 A.M.

When Jack stepped outside of The Cask & Glass, the flood of light blinded him. He used the hand holding the broom to shield his eyes. When his retinas adjusted, Jack saw a cluster of what appeared to be Middle Eastern women glaring at him through their burkas. After they spoke, Jack realized that they were actually Japanese assassins.

Ninjas! Jack panicked. He had to think quickly because ninjas could be extremely dangerous. He dropped his broom and dustpan and ran for his life in the opposite direction. He sprinted towards the park across the street and didn't look back. Jack could hear them yelling to each other as they gave chase. His heart was racing with his thoughts. He was terrified. He ran faster but didn't know how far he could sprint at that pace.

"Help me! Oh God, please help me!" Jack huffed to himself as he studied the streaking green of the grass beneath his racing feet. He ran towards the oak tree near the center of the field. Suddenly, he realized that multiple ninjas were chasing him through a park that didn't exist, for no conceivable reason. He was dreaming! Jack firmly planted his feet into the imaginary grass, stood up, and clenched his fists.

He confidently turned to face the charging assassins. His machismo caught the ninjas by surprise, even causing one of them stumble. Soon, the weaponless, black-clad warriors formed a circle around him. Jack stood tall in his work clothes—the strings of his apron flapping in the light breeze. He could see their torsos heaving as they surrounded him, catching their breath.

The first ninja charged. Jack stood on the balls of his feet and waited for the attacker's strike. The ninja dealt a high lunging punch. Jack dodged to his right, grabbed the attacker's arm with his left hand, and jerked him forward, out of balance and into Jack's firm, extended right elbow. *Smack!* The ninja was down on the grass.

That was easy. Courage raced through Jack, so he pointed at the next ninja, calling her to battle. The second assassin approached. Like a Jedi, Jack extended his arm out in the direction of the ninja. She grabbed her own throat, choking, and fell to the ground.

Unexpectedly, a dinosaur roar drowned out every other sound. The noise and tremors of the approaching colossus grew louder from behind the curtain of inner-city buildings. As it wobbled into view, the olive-colored giant was easily 20 stories tall, judging by one of the buildings he swatted in half. *Godzilla!*

Jack and the ninjas all looked up at the behemoth but remained silent. When Jack looked back to where the hit men stood, they had already vanished—synonymous with ninja behavior. Bewildered, Jack looked around and thought, *well played.*

Godzilla, sensing everything was safe, gave a giant huff and exited the scene behind a wall of buildings. Jack was left standing on the grass, looking around with a big grin on his face. He hadn't had a dream this dynamic in a long time, and he was glad he watched that ninja movie right before he fell asleep. Godzilla's presence sent it over the top and filled Jack with a sense of childhood nostalgia. It was a thrill to see his old friend once more.

Jack gauged the situation. The excitement was over. He certainly wasn't going to go back to The Cask & Glass, now. Since he was dreaming, he wanted to have some fun before he woke up and actually had to go to work. His feet started to hover as he lifted into the air. A fresh breeze pushed against his back. Fallen leaves and white feathers carried on the wind from behind him.

"Jack, wait!" She yelled over the wind. Jack fell from the air and hit the grass with a thud. He pushed himself up and looked around. To his right, Wings stood in the grass, wearing a white, v-neck t-shirt, khaki pants, and no shoes. Her dark hair was in a small bun, with a couple of loose strands blowing in the breeze.

"Hey," she murmured.

"Hey, two nights in a row," Jack replied. Wings looked around.

"This is a lovely dream, Jack. Don't you work right over there?" She nodded to The Cask & Glass and her face lit up as she remembered why she was there. She changed the subject, "Aren't you excited? Tonight, is the night!" she said. Jack just looked puzzled. "Jack, don't you remember? No more dreams! I'm going to be real. We're all ready." It was obvious that Jack was getting uncomfortable. Wings tried to play it down, "Honestly, I thought you'd be a little more excited." She rested her hands on her hips and smiled.

Jack recalled the grocery store from the night before— Wings covered in ice. He was overwhelmed. He had the option to drop it, but he just wasn't up for his mind playing tricks on him, and he wanted to take a stand. He'd already had a long enough real day.

"I know. I remember now, but what are we actually talking about? Because, seriously, you're starting to freak me out. Or technically, I'm freaking myself out? I'm just a little freaked out right now. Let's talk about how insane these dialogues have become."

"Dialogues? What the hell are you talking about? I'm as real as they come, Jack. This is all actually happening, mister!" The beautiful, young woman insisted.

"No, it's not! This is a dream. You are a dream." Jack shouted, then paused.

"Stop being a cynic. It's not like you. Just believe in me. It can be done, and if everything works out, then we'll be happy! But right now, it just sounds silly and I don't want to explain."

"Bullshit, this is just a game, a psychologically unhealthy chess match."

"Jack, how can you say that? Don't start worrying about your mental health now! I don't want to tell you." Wings pleaded. He waited and said nothing. Her face became saturated with frustration. Jack remained silent. You could hear the leaves on the oak tree rustling in the void between them.

"Fine," Wings said, "Here it goes…souls are eternal. Dreams are like the doorway for our souls to travel between the realms of life and death. Did you know that the sensation of being in a dream is identical to the afterlife? That's because when your body is asleep, your soul is free to cross-over back and forth into this imaginary world. The big difference is—when you're a full-time spirit, like me— you don't have a body. I'm stuck here, and I have to wait for you to cross-over. I can be reborn, but the line is long, and I would probably lose you. I shouldn't be real without being reborn, but I did some research and found a clause that lets me work around that."

"Did you just tell me that you're a ghost?"

"Yeah," Wings casually replied. This was a much more intricate explanation than Jack expected to hear, considering Wings' typically adorable rhetoric. He was both shocked and entertained. Jack put his arm around crazy, little Wings, and kissed her on the forehead to show he wasn't scared. It wasn't working, and he was intent on moving past the subject.

"See, that wasn't so hard," Jack said, then sarcastically thought about waking up and visiting a psychiatrist. He chuckled out loud.

"What's so funny? That was difficult for me. You don't care that I'm a ghost?"

"Of course not. You can be whatever you want. I, on the other hand, may need to see a doctor." Wings pushed him away. She gave him a serious look, but Jack was still smiling.

"You don't believe me, do you, Jack? You told me last night that you loved me, that it was *real* love! How will you recognize me if you don't believe I'm there? You need an open heart for this."

"Wings, let's just pretend that you *didn't* claim my soul was in some place other than inside of my body and skip forward to when you said you're a ghost!" He took a breath, and she interjected.

"Miracles— even curses—are real. They don't need your permission to exist. Certain days, times, and conditions can produce them, and if you're a spirit who's paying attention, you can be a part of one of those moments."

"I don't get it. Do you intend to transform from an imaginary ghost into a real ghost? Do I need a spectrometer and earphones when we hang out? Or should I just whip out my Ouija board?"

"Don't be ridiculous, Jack. It's totally not going to be like *Poltergeist*, at all. Think of it more like Patrick Swayze—you know, in *Ghost*, how he jumps into Whoopi Goldberg's body?"

"Oh, so you can possess people, too!"

"No. I mean, it's not the same. I'm not there floating around. I get placed with one body, whoever that is will be permanent, and I don't get to choose. I may be a part of their subconscious, but I will be there. They will feel me inside them, while I will feel the world through their body, and we will be one. Together, we'll find you. That's why you must believe that I'm going to do all I can to get us together—but if you reject this person, or don't try, I'll be stuck with them, and without you." Jack realized he wasn't getting the answers he wanted, so he tried something different.

"Oh, so this is Paradise, huh? What's your favorite part about being dead?"

"Are you patronizing me?"

"Are you being ironic? I'm just trying to get to the bottom of this."

Wings' frustration drained into her voice, "I like being able to communicate with the spirits of the small animals, Jack, it is my absolute favorite thing. I don't expect you to understand, but they're so adorable. Can we please drop this?"

"Sure, so how did you die?"

"I don't remember. Please stop interrogating me. I love you, Jack. I want to be real so I can be there to help you. Please, can we just drop this?"

"Help me?! You're helping me have a damn nervous breakdown!" Jack was angry.

"You don't know possible from impossible!" Wings shouted. "I'll worry about that. Tomorrow, I'm going to wake up in the body of someone close to you. I will come and find you. If you believe, you will feel me looking at you. I promise. Your questions are complicating the simplest part of a very complex thing."

"Oh, well, I'm not sorry," Jack paused, recognizing what an asshole he had become. His agitation was more than Wings could take. She was a sweet girl with good intentions, and she was under a lot of stress, already. She covered her face with her hands and began to cry. Jack just watched, unsure of what to do.

"You see, Jack!" she wept, "This is why I didn't want to tell you! Why couldn't you just drop it like I'd asked? It's not supposed to start like this! I'm a girl, so I'll find a girl, but there is no guarantee of what's going to happen next. This may be our last few minutes together...ever.

I put a lot of work into this, and now, I'm about to take a chance for our future," she choked back some tears to speak, "You, my love! You stand there, and mock me? You treat me like I'm a fucking idiot. I can't explain it to you because you are not supposed to understand. Your skepticism is part of being alive, but it hurts. If you were like me, you would understand."

Wings regained her composure. During the past few moments, the leaves of the oak tree had turned into feathers and were blowing into the air. The seasons turned from spring to summer, fall to winter, and back to spring. Wings rubbed her eyes again—they were puffy from crying.

"You see that door?" She pointed to the east with her left hand, where a doorway made of tree limbs suddenly appeared. Through it, juxtaposed against the daylight of the surrounding dream world, was the night sky. "That's the doorway to the real world. Accept it or not, I'm too close— I'm doing this. It would mean so much to me if you could stop being a jerk for these last few minutes and be that person inside of you…the man I love. The guy who still believes in long shots—who has hope. It's like you chased it away when I needed it most!" She exclaimed in disappointment, as she walked towards and stood in front of the wooden archway. Behind her silhouette was the night sky, filled with the constellations of the real world. She gazed through the doorway.

Jack began to regret almost everything he had said, "Hey, I'm sorry if I've hurt your feelings. You know what? I'll believe it when I see it—I promise. Do you know how to get to my place?" She looked at the real world, then looked back, and smiled.

"Yeah, Jack, I know where it is. I can see it, right down there. Wish me luck."

"Hey…take your shoes off before you come in!" he yelled. "I don't need all that mud on the carpet. I vacuumed this morning."

She giggled, "I know." She grabbed the door. It made a long, squeaking sound as she pulled it closed. *Skweeeeee…*

Crack! The thunder woke Jack. It was almost one in the morning and too warm for snow—regardless, a single flake

53

fell through the rain.

Jack had been asleep on the couch. The TV was still on. He grabbed his things and turned off the electronics, then headed towards the back of the flat, and into his room. After getting ready for bed, he turned off the light and stepped out onto the balcony to have a smoke. In the darkness underneath the flapping canvas overhang, he watched the sky and thought about the epic dream he'd just woken from.

The wet concrete chilled his bare feet. He watched the moonlit rain as the sound of drizzle chimed everywhere. Thunder rumbled. Jack looked west—a tiny string of lightning started in the southern sky. It jumped in jagged streaks across the clouds northward for miles, illuminating everything...including the fifty-pound vulture perched in the corner, who had just been tragically possessed by a love-sick ghost.

Squawk-hiss! came from the vulture's beak. Jack jumped back towards his door. The thunder from the distant lightning sizzled and cracked.

Jack paused for a moment of shock and confusion. "Fuck you!" he finally shouted at the bird. The vulture angled her neck out from the darkness. Her feathers were black and clumpy, dripping with the fruits of the pluvial night sky. "Are you trying to give me a damn heart attack?" Jack exclaimed. *Is this bird trying to kill me?* He thought. "What the hell do you want from me?" He asked the cold, wet creature. *This bird doesn't speak English. Why am I talking to a bird?* The vulture did not answer. She looked at Jack and inched closer to him. He inched backward. *What's going on, here?* He thought for a moment, then stared into her eyes. He hoped to see through them, to unfold something that he was missing. He knew she came from the park, but she was here for a reason, and it was probably something obvious. He stared empathetically at the dark, creepy bird. She was freezing, probably lost, and hungry.

Jack went inside the apartment, walked to the kitchen, and grabbed a chicken leg from the bucket of KFC, then returned outside. Feeding the animal made Jack feel like Saint Francis. The possessed, escaped vulture squawked. "Listen," Jack interrupted, "I don't know where you came from and why you had to land on my balcony. I don't care. If you are stalking me, I want you to know, I'd rather be stalked by something fluffy, like a squirrel." Jack tossed the drumstick on the ground in front of the vulture. She smelled it and began to eat. She was famished. Jack smiled, "Eat up, you ugly bitch, and get the fuck out of here." The bird looked up at him with pure loathing and devastation in her eyes.

Jack tried to ignore it, and went back into the living room, making sure to completely shut and lock the balcony door. Then, he finally got into bed. He knew he should call someone about the bird, but it was too late at night. As he laid in the darkness, he thought about the whole day. Jack took a sharp breath and gripped his blanket, then laid there and listened to the rain and thunder. His heartbeat slowed. He would need his energy—Friday, the 13th of August, 2006 had just begun. Insert chapter eight text here. Insert chapter eight text here.

CHAPTER 13
COLLISION COURSE, 9:00 A.M.

As she closed the door behind her, Layla Bucholtz carried a handbag over her shoulder. A large camera hung around her neck. She'd been raised in upstate New York, and three weeks ago, she graduated from the University of Pennsylvania with a degree in photography. Her father was from London, so she had spent several summers growing up in England—it was a natural destination for her to spend time in after finishing college. Back in the States, she had taken an upcoming internship with Getty Images in New York City. She started in a couple weeks. She hadn't found a place to live yet, which was making her anxious. Leaving her friend, Amber's, house, Layla thought about getting a new haircut while watching her distorted reflection in the doors of the elevator. It was her last full day in London with her friends and camera. She wasn't sure where—or with whom—to spend her time.

The doors opened, and Dustin Switch and Bridget Kenny waited to see who was getting on the elevator with them. Dustin was startled—initially thinking Layla was a member of the paparazzi—but he quickly recovered and began to play with his phone. "I just love your hair," Bridget casually commented, attempting to start a conversation with

Layla in the cramped elevator.

"Thanks. You know, that's funny. I was just thinking of getting a haircut."

"No! It's gorgeous."

"Thank you. It's just…I've had it like this for so long! Who does your hair?"

Ding! said the elevator.

"I get mine done at work. Let me give you a card! I'm a hair stylist," Bridget replied with excitement.

"Her hair is fine," Dustin said, and then looked at Layla, "Your hair is fine. All you're going to do by cutting it is fuck it up." Layla and Bridget gave Dustin a look that said, *you're an asshole*. He was familiar with the glare.

"Here's my card," Bridget said as they stood outside the elevator. Layla decided she would make a photo journal for the day and snapped her first picture.

The phone rang six times before Jack got out of bed to answer it.

"You suck!" said Dustin through the phone.

"This is Jack, sorry I missed your call. Please leave a message…*Beep!*"

"Schmuck, I know you don't have an answering machine. I got a part in a feature film. I am leaving Sunday. The plan is, we get drunk and loud on Saturday. I'll bank role the whole thing."

"Agreed," said Jack. "Where at?"

"Hyde Park. 2:00 P.M."

"What part?"

"Anti-Semitic cop, *The Blob 2*."

"No, not what role in the movie. Which part of the park?"

"Oh, um, remember that bridge where that goose attacked me?"

"Yeah, which mustache are you growing for the movie?"

"Maybe the Chaplin? Have to talk to Ronnie, first. The train's here."

After Jack got off the phone with Dustin, he found a

used condom next to the couch. It was not there when he had woken up the night before, so he logically concluded that Bridget and Kevin had sex on the sofa. Either way, cleaning up another man's used condom is as bad as it sounds. He read two chapters in his book, trying to forget the abused rubber, and left for work early, around 3:30.

Since Jack was single and desperate, he chose his clothes carefully—especially when he planned on going out after work. He decided on tan, boot cut, corduroy pants with a white, short-sleeved, button-up shirt, and blue Converse sneakers. He wore one white sock and one black sock (which was a conscious decision), a white belt, and no underwear. He clipped his keys to his back, right belt loop with a carabiner. On his left wrist, he wore several rubber bands, and on his right wrist, he wore a grey sweatband. In his pockets, he had a (British) bankcard, (Florida) driver's license, phone card, £60 cash, his library book, a pack of gum, a toothpick, and a wet nap. Under his arm, he carried a fitted, grey, dinner jacket, which he could wear if he got too cold, or to make the outfit look nicer than it actually was.

The vulture was waiting for Jack when he left his apartment that afternoon, but he didn't notice. She had followed him all the way to the shops. At a camera store and internet café, he stopped to check his email, see where the hell the vulture had come from, and what he should do if it followed him home again after work.

While online, he saw that his brother, Joey, had just eaten over six pounds of horseshoe sandwiches at the Illinois State Fair. Regarding the vulture, he found the Royal Society for the Protection of Birds (RSPB). Jack didn't have a cell phone, so he copied down the number in his notebook, so he could call them while he was at work. Next, he looked up news about missing vultures. He immediately found an article on the BBC News website about an African Vulture, named "Bones," who was reported missing by the Blackbrook Zoological Park, that Monday. She had apparently gnawed through the net of her enclosure and escaped. Jack looked up the number for the zoo and wrote it down. Afterward, he settled-up with the clerk and started the next leg of his trip to work. He was thoroughly pleased with himself—so much so, in fact, you'd think he had solved some sort of profound mystery instead of merely completing a rudimentary internet search using the words "vulture" and "London."

Elsewhere, Layla Bucholtz stood under the awning of XO Hair Salon. She looked through the pictures on her camera—Dustin and Bridget, a blue and red Paddington Station sign, the sun-struck dust of the station, the skyscrapers above the flats of Victoria, blue and yellow tulips, Big Ben, an old grey mortar and stone church, a red double-decker bus, her blue shoes on pavement, and finally a picture of the black and white awning of XO Hair Salon— the colorful images filled the screen.

Layla went inside and met her acquaintance from the elevator. Bridget talked like a machine gun about her morning, as she escorted Layla to a seat. "So, what are you thinking?" Bridget asked.

"My hair?" Layla replied, "I don't know, surprise me." Bridget went silent, which was a rare occurrence.

"I have an idea!" Bridget yelped. "Can I cut your hair to look like a picture I've seen?"

"Oh, that sounds so fun!" Layla commented, "Tell me about it."

Bridget described the drawing, and then the style of the haircut. Unable to stop sharing, she also included a description and brief psychological profile of Jack with the story. Layla took pictures of herself in the mirror while Bridget cut, colored, and chatted. An hour and a half later, Bridget was finished, and Layla loved her new look. Caught up in the sisterly euphoria of a good haircut, the two schemed and agreed that it was in Layla's best interest as a photographer to go get a drink and take some pictures at Jack's work.

As she left XO—catching her new reflection in the glass storefronts—Layla experienced an external transformation. She casually window-shopped her way to The Cask & Glass.

The real Wings was trapped inside the vulture. She saw this impersonator walking towards the pub, smiling with her camera, and rage, grief, and jealousy consumed her mind. From her perch, Bones let out a fierce squawk-hiss, which simultaneously stopped Layla in her steps and removed the smile from her face. It also notified everyone within forty meters of the pub of the creature's presence.

CHAPTER 14
A FEW MINUTES 'TIL SEVEN, 6:55 P.M.

It was 6:56 P.M. on Friday the 13th, when Keith "Hampo" Hampton abruptly grabbed his chest—his face was drenched in terror. The cell phone in the breast pocket of his blue, wool jacket vibrated, and then rang. As the jingles grew louder, the people around him heard and waited for him to answer it. It was his wife, Audrey, calling. "I'm a dead man!" He said, frantically, "I was supposed to be home an hour ago, with a chicken dinner!" He apprehensively removed the phone from his jacket, as if it were going to explode.

"Ah rubbish, Hampo! Would you pull it together?" Bruce insisted.

"But it's Audrey!"

"Just answer the bloody thing. It's giving us a headache."

Keith timidly answered the phone.

"Hello, my love," he cupped his ear with his free hand and walked outside. The Cask & Glass was loud with chatter.

Jack watched the other patrons as he pulled a pint of Best Brew for a man wearing a tan business suit with a thinning comb-over. There was a mix of about twelve regulars and several new faces forming a shoulder-to-shoulder crowd. Jack's stomach rumbled at the thought of the sandwich he made before coming to work. His taste buds sang the ingredients in his mind.

Ring-ring, ring-ring! The phone in the back room, muffled by the chatter of the customers, began to sound. Jack stopped dreaming about his sandwich, sat the beer on the counter, and collected the £5 from the man in front of him. *Ring-ring, ring-ring!* Jack turned back from the cash register to hand the man his change.

"Cheers," the man said, nodding. *Ring-ring!*

"Jack?" Mike Walsh shouted from upstairs, checking if Jack was going to answer the phone. Jack shouted back,

"I got it!" leaning on the corner wall. *Ring-ring!*

"Good evening. This is The Cask & Glass, Jack speaking."

"Oiy, Jack. It's Carrie!" It was Dustin's girlfriend and she sounded frazzled. She'd never called Jack's work before, so he was concerned.

"Hi there, Carrie. Is everything okay?"

"Have you seen Dustin? We got in a fight last night, and…"

"No, I haven't seen him."

"…and he told me that he was going to stay with you!" Jack thought quietly for a moment, not sure how to respond. Carrie interrupted the awkward silence with a sniffle, then said, "Oh, he's such a jerk! It's over!" She concluded in defeat. "Sorry to bother you, Jack. You have a good day, okay?"

"Okay, Carrie. You-" He could hear her voice crackle as she began to cry, "…too." She hung up the phone. Immediately, Jack felt awful for her—as he often did for Dustin's girlfriends. He noticed a half-pint of ale from the start of his shift that he had left sitting on the ledge next to the phone. He grabbed it with a sigh. The metal bells rang as the front door opened, and again as the door closed.

"Aye, Jack!" Keith called from the parlor, "I thought you should know that there's a bloody vulture flying around outside The Cask & Glass. You may want to ring the RSPB."

Well, that's fucking impossible, thought Jack, as he marched back into the bar, dumbfounded and eager. He pulled the glass from his lips with a mouthful of ale on the back of his throat. He didn't notice the young lady standing on the other side of the bar from him with a camera, until she said,

"I saw it, too, Jack! It looked like it wanted to kill me." Jack's head turned to the left and his eyes met Layla Bucholtz with her new hair cut—an introduction which caused him to momentarily break with reality, trying to figure out if he was dreaming or not. A short-lived sensation, he was instantly and firmly placed back into the truth of the moment by the beer in his throat…on which, he began to choke. It was 7:00 P.M.

CHAPTER 15
7:00 P.M.

Layla's new haircut was black, cut medium-length, with long, uneven bangs that fell across her face like black, clumpy icicles, and covered her fair skin when she looked down. Her eyes were a dazzling green and reminded Jack of wet Lifesavers candy.

She immediately recognized Jack from the description that Bridget gave her: average height, short hair, the only person in the bar under the age of 40 (besides herself). She thought about taking a picture, but she wanted to savor the moment of messing with this stranger's mind. She didn't imagine that he would start choking. The sounds coming from Jack while he was hunched over coughing were wretched.

One by one, people began to stare. Curly asked Jack if he was okay. Jack just put his hand up like he was asking for a time-out. Layla, feeling partly responsible, quickly planted her foot on the brass rail at the base of the bar. She boosted herself over the bar, then gave him two slaps on the back. It worked! Jack burped and began to regain his composure. His face was red.

The gang was now watching Layla. While she lurched over the bar, she smiled, then grabbed a glass and served

Jack a pint of water from the tap. Still embarrassed, he reached for the glass and Layla drew back to the customers' side of the pub. Trying to capitalize on the irony of the moment, Jack slid her a £1 coin from his pocket and took a few gulps of water, thinking about what to do next. A couple of people who caught the gesture chuckled while others extended Layla their gratitude for saving the bartender.

"Thank you," Jack added, as he gathered the remainder of his wits. The vulture was still outside, and since Jack survived, some people turned their attention to having a proper look at the rare bird.

Jack turned his attention to Layla, "I'll be right with you." Then, he faced Keith, who was patiently waiting for him to stop coughing so that he could address the giant bird outside. "It's okay, Keith. Actually, the bird's name is Bones. It escaped from the Staffordshire Zoo. It's harmless, but I'll call the RSPB while I'm on my break."

The people who were listening gave him a curious look and waited for an explanation of how he knew the information that he had just shared. Sensing this, Jack shrugged his shoulders and declared openly, "I read the news." He returned his focus to Layla, "I'm sorry about the wait. What can I get for you?"

"You read the news?"

"It's a long story."

"Clearly," Layla said. "Well, I'll have a large glass of that (pointing at the Spitfire Ale) and a bag of sour cream and onion crisps." Jack smiled. Layla unsnapped her wallet and looked at Jack, waiting for the total.

"If you'd like to sit down, I'll bring it around to you," he said.

"Okay, but how much?"

"On the house."

"Ha! My lucky day." Layla laughed, "Okay, is it alright for me to sit outside? That bird is harmless, right?"

"That's what the news says."

Mike Walsh, the manager, entered through the doorway from the back room. "Heavens, Jack!" Mike crowed, "Are you okay? I heard you all the way upstairs! I thought I was about to lose another barman." Mike's voice rose, holding back a laugh that almost sounded like a gasp for air, "Pretty good crowd tonight. The gang's all here, aye? Jack, it's about time for your break." This meant Jack was on break. Mike surveyed the pub.

"Simply terrific," Mr. Novak said, after he pulled the curtain back, peered out of the window, and watched Bones flying in circles.

"It's ghastly," one woman said, as Layla walked past her.

"What a dreadful beast!" another exclaimed, filing in from the street.

Layla looked back and noticed Jack taking money from his wallet to buy her drink and chips. When she turned around, she was outside.

Friday's clear skies erased most of the signs of Thursday's rainstorm. The early-evening sun looked like a glowing tangerine above the sharp lines of the buildings. Layla sat down at the farthest of the three outside tables from the door. She never imagined that she would see a vulture in London. *Snap.* The camera shutter clicked a picture of Bones as she took a perch on a parapet across the street. The possessed bird looked down at Layla, again. There was an undeniable intensity of the bird's focus on the photographer. Layla took one more picture before a definitively eerie feeling began to wash over her. She rested her camera on the table and waited for Jack.

CHAPTER 16
THANKSGIVING, 7:05 P.M.

Jack stepped outside. He was carrying a tray with two plates, each featuring half a sandwich and a bag of crisps. He wasn't completely naïve to the fact that his wildest dream may have just come true. However, somewhere inside, Jack was a realist. The reality was simply that a cute girl had finally shown up at his work and he was lucky to be going on his break while she was there—it was only a potential opportunity, nothing more. More importantly, this moment would require him to act like a sane, adult man in order to capitalize on it.

The two made eye contact. Then, Layla looked up towards Bones, and back at Jack. He shrugged his shoulders. Layla quickly raised her camera and snapped a picture, smiled, and rested her equipment back on her lap.

Jack smiled and enquired, "Could I ask you a couple questions?"

"Okay," she calmly replied.

"First, may I join you?"

"Sure."

"Awesome! Second, are you a vegetarian?" He took the open seat and set the tray down, then handed her a sandwich plate with chips and her drink.

"Not really. Does it have chicken?" she inquired.

"Yes." He looked confused.

"I don't eat chicken. Thank you, though."

"Fascinating," Jack said, watching his brilliant "sharing-of-a-meal" idea go down in flames. He grabbed the sandwich off her plate and placed it back on his. "Okay, one more question: what's your name?" Layla drew her hand to her chest. She had completely forgotten that he knew nothing about her. She laughed at herself and apologized.

"Sorry, my name is Layla. This vulture is so wild! It's just staring at us."

"Yeah, it could definitely be perceived that way. Thanks again, Layla."

"It wasn't a big deal. I just gave you a slap on the back."

"Oh, the choking! I would have been fine. I was thanking you for coming into the pub. This place gets extremely *old* some days."

Layla chuckled as Jack took a bite of his chicken sandwich. He chewed with satisfaction, swallowed, and took a sip of beer.

"So, off the record," he said, "You don't eat chicken?"

"Pretty much," Layla confirmed. "When I was a kid, one night I stayed up late to watch Saturday Night Live like the other kids in school, when the "Clucking Chicken" skit came on. Since it started as a cartoon, I was really excited because I didn't understand the other jokes. Well, when they put poor Cluckin' through the chicken factory and he was dismembered, I was horrified and started crying. I didn't know how chicken was made! I've had nightmares about being one of those poor chickens ever since."

"Well," Jack added, "I had a dream once, where a group of pigs in togas attacked me like I was Julius Caesar. The eeriest thing was that it happened on the Ides of March. Though the writing may be on the wall, so to speak, I didn't stop eating bacon."

Squawk-hiss! interrupted the vulture, shaking her feathers.

Jack continued, "You know, chicken is one of the most, if not the most, succulent and delectable entrées in the entire solar system…possibly the galaxy. My point here is only that I selectively believe in the dreams that inspire me, not the nightmares that scare me shitless. Dreams can hold you back just as much in the same ways that they can propel you forward in life, but ultimately the choices are ours, and the dreams are just dreams."

Layla interjected, "I meant to ask about that vulture watching us. Is it following you?" She ate a crisp from the plate as she watched Jack savor his lunch. He put his finger up to signal that he would further explain Bones, in a moment. "You're pretty passionate about your sandwich."

"I have my reasons." Jack said, covering his half-full mouth.

Layla took her half of the sandwich back from his plate and sunk her teeth into it. "Holy crap! This is awesome," she said instantly, with purple cranberry sauce on her teeth. "It tastes like Thanksgiving!" She chewed for a moment. "Is that stuffing and cranberry sauce?"

"It is," Jack watched awestruck, "What changed your mind?"

"I'm not sure, I haven't been myself all day," Layla said, then winked, as she prepared to take another bite.

CHAPTER 17
LOVE BIRDS, 7:27 P.M.

It was a Saturday afternoon. Lenard and Jack were together, shopping for Carol's birthday present at Daytona Beach's Volusia Mall. When Lenard noticed Jack staring at a pretty, little girl with blonde hair, he decided it was a good time to give his youngest son some relationship advice.

"Jack, you think that little blonde girl in the pink dress is cute?" Jack nodded his head. Lenard could tell Jack was a little embarrassed. "Remember this, son: take a look at her mom. She is downright gruesome! That's a bad sign, my boy." Jack looked confused. Lenard continued, anyway. "You see, son, beauty is nice, but it all goes to shit. The price of being young and beautiful is growing old and being ugly. Don't just chase a pretty girl. Chase a girl that makes you laugh, think, and care about the world. Whether you get those girls, or not, the pursuit of them can make you a better person."

Jack and Layla sat outside The Cask & Glass. They talked about the various nuances of European telephones, as she took a picture of two pigeons. It was 7:28 P.M. and the hues of the sky were settling into dusk. The vulture watched from her perch across the street, while bellowing voices escaped through the swinging front door of Jack's workplace. The light inside gave the windows an orange glow.

"You know, Jack, I think that there's a conspiracy to

make hold music intentionally as annoying as possible," Layla said. Her glass was empty. "I believe when a company doesn't want to deal with a customer, they put them on hold until the person gets so frustrated that they hang up."

"Agreed." Jack picked up the conversation, "This one time, it was like a horror movie..." Layla started laughing because she could tell he was being sarcastic. "...Forty-five minutes of the same, crackling, 1930's jazz record. Then, all of a sudden, the music changed to wild industrial sounds and a demonic voice that shouted 'Hang-up!' then back to the jazz." Jack finished and cocked his brow, patiently waiting for a response.

"Did you know, they actually sit there and listen to you waiting on hold?" Layla asked, and then began to mimic one of the employees who monitor the people on hold having a discussion with their boss. "Sir, I need some help. You know, the rebate?" Jack jumped in, playing the part of the demanding boss, as they began to improvise,

"Jesus, Carl! You haven't authorized any rebates, have you?"

"No! No! I don't want to lose my job," she said.

"You nearly gave me a heart attack. What's the problem?"

"Currently, we have a dingleberry on line 3 who won't let go. They have all fourteen forms of proof of purchase..."

Jack feigned disbelief, "The dated newspaper *and* original birth certificate?"

"All of them," She confirmed. They stopped to laugh at each other and continued the scene.

"Damn it! What hold music have you got them plugged into?" Jack asked, taking a sip of beer.

"Middle-school flute and violin practice: two-minute loop," she replied. Jack dramatically spit out some of the beer, then quickly said.

"They *are* tenacious! Okay. Here's the plan. Just take them off hold, and then blow this modified dog whistle. It should make them nauseous and disoriented. Then, put them back on hold while I go get my Jock Jams 8 CD from my car."

"You're going to let the dogs out?"

"I have no choice!"

They couldn't go any further. For the next few minutes, they just laughed and repeated themselves. Their laughter cascaded together, and Jack's cheeks hurt from being so high on his face. He couldn't see—his eyes were squinted and filled with little tears. Using his palms like windshield wipers, Jack swiped away the salty droplets. He could hear Layla catching her breath. Before he opened his eyes, he felt different…no, nervous about something. Jack sat back and watched Layla, then leaned back and saw the vulture still watching them. He had forgotten to call the RSPB. Layla was about to leave, and he may never see her again, and he was late getting back to work!

Hastily, he asked Layla what her plans were for the evening. She told him about going out with her friends, then asked him if he was interested in coming out after his shift. It was the easiest answer he had ever given.

"May I bring the bird?"

"Okay." She laughed and passed him a homemade business card from her wallet. "After work, just catch the underground to Piccadilly Circus and call me." Layla collected her stuff and started walking towards the station. She turned around and waved to Jack. While he waved back, she lifted her camera and took another picture.

Jack smiled as he collected the plates and glasses from both tables. His mind was lovesick with speculation. *Did she want to kiss me like I wanted to kiss her? Where would we kiss? What type of kiss would it be? Are we going to get really drunk? Should I ever mention that she looks just like the girl from my dreams, or will that weird her out? Am I going to get some ass? Should I bring a condom? She said that she liked poetry. Should I write her a poem? Is that too creepy? How much will I talk about myself? What really great story should I tell her? How should I act with her friends? If she gets pregnant, I'll ask her to marry me. Holy shit! What am I thinking about? Jesus, Jack, what's wrong with you? Get back to work!*

CHAPTER 18
CLOCKING OUT, 9:15 P.M.

Layla and Bones had won the interest of the group of regulars at The Cask & Glass. During the last bits of the night, Jack's patrons interrogated him like a drunken hydra with an English accent. While Jack finished his chores, the inquiry culminated in a semi-coherent onslaught of questions.

"So, when are you meeting the little flower?" Bruce asked.

"I believe her Christian name is Layla," said Andrew with his arm over Bruce's shoulder. Jack looked up at them.

"Oh, did you see old Jack's eyes light up when you said her name?! Layla."

"Oh, yeah, look at that! Like a bloody Christmas tree," Andrew prodded. Jack gave them both a stern look, and then smiled. They grinned back. Martin seemed to be stewing on something over in his seat. Jack stacked the last chair and walked back behind the bar.

He felt Mary staring at him before she spoke, "So, Jack," she asked, "when do you head back to the States?"

"Well, after my vacation in Greece, I suppose."

"Oh, I love Greece! Did you enjoy your time here in London? It's really a splendid city, isn't it?" Jack gave an affirming nod. Mary initiated this exact same dialogue nearly every night sometime after her third glass of wine.

"Are you taking your pet (vulture) to Greece?" Andrew asked.

"Only if she buys her own ticket," Jack quickly replied.

"Unflappable as usual, Jack," Bruce said with a smile. Mary was drunk. Martin looked stern.

"I think you should be taking this bird more seriously," Martin said, then finished his fourth glass of scotch.

"Oh, bollocks," Bruce objected.

"Why am I the only one who sees that there is something wrong with that bird? That foul creature has been out there for hours for no reason! Doesn't it make you think? It doesn't make you concerned? Is all you can do laugh and carry on about it like idiots?"

"Martin, I agree. There is something fowl in the air," Andrew declared, patronizing Martin with his avian pun.

"Indeed!" Bruce said in agreement with Andrew. It took Martin a moment to catch the pun. He was both surprised and hurt that nobody took him seriously. Furthermore, being laughed at made him extremely upset—his blood pressure rose, and his face turned red. Bruce and Andrew were laughing too hard to notice. Bruce gave a hardy snort, getting Mary's attention, but she was still completely oblivious to the entire situation.

"Hey... hey. What are you worried about, Marty?" Andrew caught his breath. "We aren't chickens!" Bruce's beer jostled around in the bottom of the bottle as his hand held it on top of the bar. Martin placed his glass down on the table in front of him with a smack, stood up, grabbed the door, the bells jingled twice, and he was gone.

"Oh Martin, don't get so bent out of shape, we're just taken' the piss," Bruce said to Andrew, since Martin had already left. "Well, that's old Marty for you—so serious. He's going to blow a gasket, someday. Tragic, really."

"Well, Jack," Andrew said, "According to our friend, Martin, it looks like we're doomed. Do you have any last words?" This question caused a brief moment of silence. Bruce spoke, first.

"Last words?" Bruce repeated, "I'd say, 'A toast! To better days!'" Bruce dangled his tongue out onto his big cheek and played dead.

"Ah, that's an excellent set, Bruce!" Andrew laughed.

"What are you two going on about?" Mary asked, with glassy eyes.

"Oh nothing, dear Mary," Bruce replied.

Jack thought about his last words for a moment. When he knew he had everyone's attention, he said, "'Suicide is for cowards and prima donnas!' will be my last words…before I fly a hang-glider into the caldera of a roaring volcano." Jack paused for a second, realizing that this went over the heads of everyone. Feeling awkward, he kept talking, "But seriously, I'm tired of people being scared all the time. It's no way to live. Whatever happened to coexisting? It's just a bird. You know, not every culture sees vultures as harbingers of death. I read it, today! The Native Americans saw them as a symbol of peace. The ancient Egyptians used the vulture as a symbol of love in their hieroglyphs. In fact, I may mention that to Layla, later. I'm not too concerned about some worst-case scenario with me and this bird. It's one bird, not a flock. If the damn thing tries anything stupid, I'll break its filthy neck."

This comment brought some serious looks. Jack started to whistle the lullaby from *Lady and the Tramp* as he watched the clock strike ten. Then, he killed the main lights and said, "Sorry, ladies and gentlemen, no lollygagging tonight! I've got a date with the girl of my dreams."

Ten minutes later, a hundred meters away, streetlights shined yellow circles on the road. The vulture and the now-deceased Martin Sage rested a few blocks north of The Cask & Glass. Bones jabbed and poked at the exposed cheek of the late district attorney, keeping her wings half-open to hold her balance. His blood was still warm. She jiggled her head back and shook the torn chunks of flesh into her mouth and down her throat.

"Oh my God!" *Eeeeeek!* The scream came from behind Bones, interrupting her meal. She furiously hissed at the intruder and jumped into flight with only a mouthful of Mr. Sage. She flapped and gained altitude, then soared north towards Piccadilly, where Jack would head after closing up the pub.

Several blocks away, Jack was giddy. He looked at the city stars through the smoke from his cigarette—random lights illuminated the shimmering, dark, glass walls of the office towers. He whistled *Strangers in the Night* to himself as he walked southeast toward Victoria Station. The girlish scream distracted him and caused him to miss a beat.

Still no vulture, he thought. After two days, he had become accustomed to the bird. It seemed harmless, and he liked the attention. He'd been abnormally chatty all day. As he got to the station, a day-dream-like vision of Wings flickered in front of him, which caused a personal conflict to come to a head. He gave himself a pep-talk.

This is no time to be thinking irrationally, Jack. Be a man, for Christ's sake. If you bring your weird dreams into this situation, you're going to fuck it up! There is no room for error. This is not an opportunity to prove that you are a lunatic. The shopping cart is full of crazy shit and we need to make a little room in that cart for some pussy, hombre. Remember to listen first, and only speak when you have something interesting or funny to say. Be honest, but not gushy. Stay calm and be yourself, and you won't have any regrets. Jack pushed Wings to the back of his mind as he found clarity in a plan. He knew exactly what his first move would be.

He swiped his travel card and walked through the turnstile. The train arrived as Jack approached the track, and he coasted aboard it without breaking his pace. The train was full of silent people. Jack took the cue and removed his book from his jacket before taking a seat. He started Chapter 8 as the train jolted up to speed. He stopped thinking, started reading, and his egocentric thoughts disappeared.

CHAPTER 19
MEANWHILE, 10:30 P.M.

"Did you and Jack have fun at The Cask & Glass?" Carrie asked Dustin in her sweetest voice when he came home.

"Huh?" Dustin replied, confused. The derailment of his train of lies had begun. "I mean, always, hot legs! How was work?"

"Get out of my fucking apartment!" She said with the sort of force that made Dustin turn around and leave without further question. While in shock, he walked to the bar on the corner and ordered six shots of tequila. After a couple of minutes, he went back to Carrie's place—substantially more drunk—to find that he was locked out and left standing in the hallway.

As Dustin began to apologize to his girlfriend's door, she opened it, threw two eggs at him—one at his chest, and the other at his head while he was looking at his chest. She slammed the door, told him she had to shit, and threatened to call the authorities if he wasn't gone by the time she'd finished. Dustin silently responded to the whole situation with his facial expressions, then turned away from the door like a scolded dog and headed for the street.

Elsewhere, Layla and her friends, Amber, Paula, Sharon,

Tristan, Alex, and Larry, were riding together on a crowded train as it quickly slowed to a stop at Piccadilly Circus. The doors slid open and live jazz music from the performers poured into the train car. Tile mosaics of flowers and people covered the walls of the station. Layla's senses began to fill with new memories. Her group merged into the centipede of people rumbling towards the exit stairs. In the squeeze of the commuters, her eyes caught an infant in a stroller. She and the baby exchanged stares, smiles, and even waves. *She's so cute*, Layla thought, wishing she had brought her camera.

They were almost outside. Layla thought about her ex-boyfriend. She wondered if Grant would like her new hair. She couldn't believe he talked her into coming to visit him at Oxford. Her phone rang. She didn't recognize the number but answered anyway.

"Hello?"

"Layla, its Jack." *It was Jack.*

"Jack! Where are you?"

"I'm in front of St. James Tavern, on Great Windmill Street."

"Let me see…where we are going." Jack could hear the crowd of people as Layla yelled to Amber. "Hey! That's where we are headed, St. James."

"How many people are you with?" Jack asked.

"Seven, but I think another guy is coming later."

"Cool, well I'll see if I can get us a table."

"Sounds good. See you soon."

PART III: SATURDAY, AUGUST 14TH, 2006

CHAPTER 20
ULTERIOR MOTIVES, 12:15 A.M.

It seemed that the neon beer signs were the only source of light in St. James Tavern. The reds, blues, greens, and dark shadows set the atmosphere. Jack had arrived before Layla and her friends. He spent seventy percent of his money within that first couple of minutes.

First, he found a suitable table. Then, he returned to the front door, gave the doorman a description of Layla and her friends, and asked him to let them know where he was sitting. To solidify the request, Jack gave the doorman a £5 note. Next, Jack went to the bar. There, he ordered a beer for himself and a round of Jägermeister shots for Layla and her friends. He asked the bartender to wait until after they arrived to bring them over. He paid for the drinks with a smile, tipped the staff (an American custom), and returned to the table. It was a little expensive, but Jack had pulled this move off once before, and he was banking on the hope that it would work again.

A few minutes later, Layla and her friends arrived. Both

the doorman, Dillon, and the waitress, Beth, handled their roles in Jack's set piece with an amazing level of showmanship; allowing Jack to not just break the ice, but to crush it.

A minute later, everyone was smiling. Amber still had her shot in her hand and Louis already had an arm over Jack's shoulder, asking him what he wanted to drink. As they settled in around the table and the alcohol got comfortable in their stomachs, the comments tangentially became discussions of a variety of topics: how the internet has turned taxidermy into a competitive global industry, Layla's new designer haircut, Jack's vulture, and how to properly garnish corndogs on a stick.

Tristan had bought everyone shots at midnight. Afterwards, half the group, including Jack, stepped out front for a cigarette. Because she checked for traffic in the wrong direction, an oncoming taxi nearly struck Sharon while she was foolishly attempting to pick up a £2 coin that had fallen on the street. Luckily, Jack was able to pull her out of the way, and everyone was grateful. Some had described Jack's reflexes as lightning-fast, even cat-like.

When the smokers returned inside, two new gentlemen were standing by the table talking to Paula and Layla. Jack also overheard Larry comment that Layla was a hot, little piece of "trim," and that he was pretty confident that she wanted "The Larester." Jack consulted himself silently. *This guy, Larry, is going to be a serious pain in my ass. Now I've got these other two fucking jabronies to deal with. We need a few more girls over here before this gets out of hand.* Jack glanced around and saw two attractive, unoccupied girls at the end of the bar.

He confided to Louis that he had a growing concern about the girl-to-guy ratio. Louis bet Jack two shots that Jack could walk up to any woman in the bar and get them to come join them. Jack laughed.

"Ha-ha! Okay, my friend," Jack said, after needing zero convincing. He looked around, drawing the same conclusion, and said, "Two o'clock."

Jack approached slowly. He was thinking about how he was going to introduce himself. Three shots of melon and vodka, and one *Nostrovia* later, he deduced (because they told him) that the young women were from Ukraine. Chloë was taking a break from law school. She was visiting Audrey, who was studying to be a nurse.

"I'd like to introduce you both to the group I'm with. They're pretty charming guys," offered Jack.

"Like you?" Audrey grinned.

Jack smiled, "Sure, they're probably not confident enough to come over and talk to you, though. Honestly, I think I'm in love with the girl in the blue shirt, over there. I just need some help keeping all the other great guys away from her so we can talk. Do you think you could help me out? It's really important."

"Ah, that is so sweet! Okay, I'll help you," said Audrey, without hesitation. Chloë looked more apprehensive. She spoke with her thick, Eastern European accent,

"I do not know; that one has kind of a weird look in his eyes."

"Who? The Larester?" Jack said, looking at Larry, who was standing about thirty meters away. Larry's face was rapidly changing expressions because he farted while squinting his eyes to read the neon dry-erase menu on the back wall.

"You're right...that is not a good look. Let's not focus on Larry. Is there anything I can do, Chloë?"

"Buy me another drink. I will come; talk to your friends; help you get girl." Jack smiled. He was on fire. The last thing he remembered was an intense feeling of bravado, as he gripped a peanut from a tray near the napkin holder on the bar.

CHAPTER 22
MISSING CHAPTERS, 8:59 A.M.

Putney is a suburb about six miles southwest of central London. It takes around forty minutes to get there by bus. The streets are broad and peppered with trees, with tall, grand houses flush to the street. The main boulevard looks like a row of tiny, elegant castles placed side-by-side.

Bones flew through the sky empty, confused, and alone, trying to find Jack. The morning wind streaked cold against her fleshy, red scalp. Below her, the pigeons that commuted from the city at night nested by the hundreds in the enormous oak trees of the neighborhood. At sunrise, their coos flowed together in a melodic river of sound.

It was 10:30 A.M. and Jack Chestnut was asleep in the bed of Terry Chapel, a twelve-year-old boy from France. Fortunately, Terry was not home. In fact, the entire Chapel family was on vacation in New Zealand. Louis, Layla's French friend, lived with the Chapels. He tutored Terry, walked the dog, baby-sat, smoked pot, went to school, and most importantly, he house-sat the Chapel's spacious residence while they were away.

Jack woke up a minute later, at 10:31. He didn't open his eyes; just assessed his gut feelings. He didn't feel any shame. In fact, it actually seemed like he had a good night, last night.

Due to couple of black outs, his memory was like a broken jigsaw puzzle.

He started reviewing the bits of what he could remember. The first thing he recalled was the bus. *It was bright. They were all rumbling down the road. The air filled with bursts of laughter in all directions, like sporadic fireworks. Jack's mouth was dry. He felt a Band-Aid sticking to his elbow. He remembered the vulture on the lamp post across the street, outside St. James Pub. He watched Sharon stroll out to get a £5 note tumbling in the road. She was looking the wrong way.*

Jack felt a bit like Goldie Locks as he opened his eyes to see the green and silver transformer toy on the pine wood desk across from the bed. The room had a vaulted ceiling. He was on the top floor, or a wing of the house, perhaps. It sounded like there were a thousand pigeons outside. From the window in the center of the triangular wall, the sun lightly toasted the *Star Wars* sheets on the bed. Jack wished he had taken his pants off before he went to bed, but remembered he wasn't wearing boxers. He stared at the ceiling, then looked at the door. Layla Bucholtz was standing in the doorway; sideways, from his perspective.

"Good morning, Hero," she said, quietly.

"Hello, Wings," Jack replied, grinning foolishly. He could feel his blood flowing and sat up.

"You shouldn't look at me like that," Layla coyly replied. "It's a giveaway that you're in love with me."

He took it in stride, "Just wait right there." He cleared his voice, taking a sarcastic and defensive tone. "I'm in love with you? You're the one who had your hair cut to look like one of my drawings. Then, came sta... sta...looking for me." Layla pretended to be shocked, and returned the tone, in kind.

"Listen. One, I didn't ask her to cut my hair to look *exactly* like your picture. She asked me. And two, I wasn't stalking you. It was part of my photo journal."

"Woah, there," he said, "One, I'm the person who counts my points." Layla laughed.

"Two, who said the word stalking? I thought we cleared that up last night." He looked over at the Transformer, "How about you, Mr. Thundercleese? Did you hear me say stalking? I believe I said, 'looking.'" He shook his head. She laughed. He continued, "And three, you're the one staring at me like *you're* in love!" He punctuated this statement with his most adorable accusatory stare.

"Shut your lying face!" She yelled, playfully. "Three, you told me that you loved me last night, remember?" Jack's face went blank, and she continued, "I had the hiccups! I told you to scare me so I would stop. Then, you said, 'I love you,' and it worked! No more hiccups. It was really funny!" He frowned, and she smiled. "Ah, you're too cute. Breakfast is almost ready! Everybody's talking about you. They're asking, 'Where's Jack?' 'Where's the hero?' So, I came to see if you were up." He smiled.

"I'm awake," he looked around, still a little bewildered, "I'll be down soon, okay?"

She smiled, turned, and disappeared into the hallway. He could hear her footsteps fade away on the carpet stairs.

In Terry's room, Jack put on his shoes, but decided to carry his jacket. Looking in the bathroom mirror, he noticed he had shaved, somehow. *When did I shave?* He decided not to worry about it. He brushed his teeth with his finger and some of Terry's sparkly toothpaste, then double-checked he didn't leave anything, before making his way into the hall.

It was Jack's first time seeing the Chapel's house in the sober colors of daylight. It looked entirely different—from what, he didn't exactly remember. The walls were painted a light shade of olive green. Large scenic photographs hung above the banister. It had an appropriately homey feeling. As he descended the staircase, a few pieces of the jigsaw puzzle fell into place.

CHAPTER 21
THEIR FIRST MISS, 3:32 A.M.

Everybody in the house was drunk, stoned, or both. Together, Jack and Layla were exploring the residence. They crawled on their bellies up the unlit staircase like they were soldiers sneaking under barbed wire. The surface leveled out when they reached the second floor. The stress of crawling a flight of stairs on their stomachs was in their breath. "I'm going in! I think the bathroom is right there." Layla said with conviction.

"Jesus, it's dark!" Jack said, "Be careful."

In the dark, Layla laughed at him, smiled, then turned and started exploring into the hallway. Jack snuck a glance at her backside—it looked fantastic. It was time to make a move. He grabbed her by the ankle and tugged her firmly backward. Her relatively light body slid to a stop next to him on the carpet. They were face to face, grinning, with their pupils wide in the darkness.

You could argue, on an emotional level, that they were already kissing. He moved his hand up her side, and over the curve of her hip onto her waist. She inched towards him. They tilted their heads, and then, the bathroom door creaked.

Larry leapt from the bathroom like a lunatic and

screamed "BOOOO!"

"Holy Fuck, Larry!" Jack exclaimed.

"You fucking asshole! I almost shit my pants," Layla added, "What the fuck is wrong with you?"

Larry responded indirectly, "Fuck, I've been waiting up here for like, twenty minutes to do that, but it was worth it! Come on, we're going to play some Perudo. Make-out time is later," Larry said, looking at Layla.

CHAPTER 23
HERO, 9:13 A.M.

"Morning, Hero," said Sharon, as she walked up the stairs, snagging Jack from his daydream and bringing him back to the present. "Thanks again for saving my life last night," she added.

"I was just trying to get that £2," Jack said. Sharon laughed, slapped him on the shoulder as she passed, and moved her hand to his neck. This was an extremely flirtatious and unexpected move, but Jack managed to stay calm.

"Nice shave," she said. Sharon removed her hand and continued up the stairs towards the bathroom.

Jack got to the bottom of the staircase and saw the front door to his left. The house was laid out in the shape of a crucifix, with the staircase in the center. Just past the coat rack in front of him was a library. The light shining in from the front window reflected off an expensive-looking, polished brown leather sofa. To the right of the stairs was a short hallway, which led to the laundry and dining rooms.

Voices came from the sunroom, so Jack followed the sound. He entered the dining room. It was a long, rectangular space. The walls were a dark, wood paneling with windows on one side and pictures on the other. A mahogany table with ten chairs and a bowl of fruit were the centerpiece. Jack touched a plum to see if it was real.

"Jack! Hello, my friend," Louis said, entering the dining room and somewhat startling Jack, "Did you sleep well?"

Jack considered the question, "I slept well. This house is incredible," he added.

"Yes, it is. Like a dream," Louis remarked, "And, no vultures!"

"Ha-ha! No vultures. La dolce vita," Jack added in Italian, for no reason.

"Parli Italiano?" Louis asked.

"No."

"Tristo, va maginito," Louis continued in Italian, anyway.

"In the kitchen?" Jack asked.

"Si," Louis confirmed, patting Jack on the back as he walked past to get his shoes from the laundry room. Tristan, Paula, and Amber sat around the glass table in the sunroom and looked pleased when Jack stepped through the doorway. The whole place smelled like a Waffle House. The kitchen counter was made of wavy, grey marble, the walls and cabinets were a cream color with white trim. The stove had two giant pads, instead of separate burners. Layla patted some bacon with a paper towel. There were also a variety of slices of bread, jellies, and even eggs—it all looked delicious.

"He-ro," Tristan started to chant.

"He-ro," Paula joined him.

"He-ro," Tristan, Paula, Amber, and Layla shouted together, and then repeated, again. Jack modestly tried to quiet them with his hands. It didn't work, so he encouraged them, instead. He whirled his arm at his elbow and then dramatically cupped his hand to his ear. He wasn't sure if everyone would get his Hulk Hogan reference, but he did it anyway. They stopped chanting and laughed.

"I love this guy," Amber said. Jack was overwhelmed by food and flattery. He walked over and gave Layla a playful kiss on the cheek, which made her purse her lips and blush.

Jack shuffled over to the sink to help wash the growing stack of dishes. He looked out over the backyard, as he scrubbed a mixing bowl. The yard was shaped like an augmented rectangle. The largest patch was past the swing set, next to a small pond. Jack noticed Alex and Larry—they were covered in grass stains and jockeying for position around a kid's soccer ball. They looked fatigued, to say the least.

"What the hell are Alex and Larry doing in the backyard?"

"Playing one-on-one soccer," Layla said, "I heard they've been up all night."

Jack finished drying a bowl and put it on the rack. "To be honest, I don't remember when, why, or how we even got here."

"Jack, I don't remember a lot of stuff, but it's been fun. We should piece it all together over brunch." Layla grinned.

"Good idea."

CHAPTER 24
DÉJÀ VU, 11:59 A.M.

Jack's hearty laugh was like a ping on the vulture's soul-seeking sonar. It was noon when Bones finally took perch on the Chapel's roof, and no one noticed. From her angle, the ground was covered with pigeon feathers and white bird shit. This was less apparent to the individuals beneath the tree's branches without an aerial view. In fact, Louis and his company didn't notice that the top surface of everything besides the picnic table they were sitting at had some degree of bird excrement splattered across it.

Alex and Larry were covered in grass stains and broken leaves. Their eyes were bloodshot and baggy. At the moment, they were playing a violent adaptation of rock-paper-scissors. In their version of the game, the loser of the round got punched in the arm. While the intensity and improbability of their competition were duly noted by the onlookers, Alex and Larry contributed very little in conversation except for the occasional yelp of pain from Larry. Alex had bested him in every competition they had been in since their game of Perudo six hours ago. It had become a ferocious and pitiful bro-cathalon. Alex continued his unbelievable streak of victories, while Larry refused to accept that even the Gods probably thought he was a douche.

Meanwhile, Jack and Layla brought the breakfast plates to the kitchen from the picnic table. Tristan, Louis, and Paula played pinochle. Sharon and Amber talked about details from the previous night. Then, both turned to Jack and said, "You bribed the bouncer?" Jack held his finger up for a pause.

"Bribed? I politely gave him money and instructions. That's the American way, sweethearts."

"Putan!" Tristan cursed in French and put his cards down. His hand was terrible, and his accent was thick. "So, my friend, that is why the doorman, he acted like he knew you."

"Okay, y'all, so he bribed the doorman, but why did the bartender bring out the shots like Jack owned the place?" asked Amber.

"Hey, did you bribe the bartender, too?"

"That wasn't a bribe!" Jack remarked, "Regardless, it was an insignificant amount. Can we please give a little credit to my charming demeanor?"

"Wow," said Paula. Jack left the table and carried a bowl of crumbs to the kitchen.

"Is that when I showed up?" Louis asked.

"Louis!" The girls screamed together, in affirmation.

"Just like Heaven came on!" Paula said, putting her winning hand of cards down on the table. Immediately, Amber and Paula both sang and danced in their seats. "'Show me!'" Sharon joined in, "'Show me/ Show me/ How you do that trick/ The one that makes me scream, she said/'" Layla joined in, returning from the kitchen. "'The one that makes me laugh, she said/ And threw her arms around my neck.'"

Meanwhile, Alex dealt paper. Larry's hand was in the shape of a fist, indicating that he had chosen rock. "'Show me how you do it/ And I promise you, I promise that/ I'll run away with you/ I'll run away with you!'"

Alex set his fist, like an archer about to let loose an

arrow, six inches away from Larry's shoulder. On the roof, Bones was starving and despondent, bitterly watching all the fun they were having, below. Layla grabbed the last of the plates.

"OMG, I...love that song, y'all!" Amber giggled.

Jack walked back to the table from the kitchen. Smack! Alex's fist collided with Larry's shoulder. All of the conversation paused in acknowledgment of the brutal sound.

"Mother Theresa!" Larry cried out. Alex laughed; Louis and Tristan cringed; the rest of the group made an earnest effort to ignore the gladiators and maintain the conversation.

"Then I bought some shots, remember?" said Tristan. Paula recoiled and said,

"Jägermeisters!"

Sharon looked at Jack, "Yup, that's when the car almost hit me, but Jack saved my life." Jack smiled, "I told you, I was just trying to get the £2 off the road, before you. I'm poor."

Sharon looked at everyone, "Well, I forgot the English drive on the opposite side of the road."

"So that is why everyone started calling him the Hero."

"That's when Jude and Kenny came over! Jude was fucking dreamy," Amber casually recollected.

"Don't remind me," Alex interjected, "I go outside for two minutes, and it starts raining douchebags!"

"Jude is on my dream team," said Sharon.

"Is that where five guys and their coach run a train on you?" Larry smugly inquired.

"That's your mother's dream team," Layla said as she flanked him, walking around the table from the kitchen. The girls found this jab amusing. Bones was not impressed. In fact, she was bloodthirsty. She hated Layla, and Larry too.

"And then, the other girls!" remembered Tristan, nodding his head, looking in Jack's direction.

"For the record," Jack began, "I wasn't trying to be a

hero. I had ulterior motives," he discreetly winked at Layla, then said, "A good girl-to-guy ratio means peace."

"You're talking about Chloë and Audrey, those Eastern Bloc babes?!" Louis remarked. "Audrey was so hot, my man." Paula looked at Louis like he had a girlfriend.

"How did you get them to come over so fast? Was it the trick you did with the peanut?" Tristan asked. Paula looked at Jack, too.

"Holy shit, I forgot about that peanut. That was actually after the fact, though. What got those ladies was more of that old-fashioned charm that I've subtly kept mentioning," Jack said, sarcastically.

CHAPTER 25
SATURDAY MORNING, 12:32 A.M.

Louis reenacted Jack's grabbing of the peanut, stretching it back into his rubber band, then shouted, "*Clang!* I can't believe that you were able to sling-shot that peanut into the tip bell, then it ricocheted back and landed in your mouth. And you winked at everyone like you knew it was going to happen. It was pretty impressive."

"That actually was pretty fucking rad," said Alex.

Jack faced the backyard but saw the memory. He said, "I remember that! It was kind of a bold move. I didn't have a choice about that peanut, though. I was just a little too excited when I let it loose, and I put too much tension on my rubber band slingshot. That nut was flying! It could have taken my eye out. Catching it in my mouth was the most conservative thing I could have done."

"Then we went to Thrillers, y'all," Amber said, skipping an hour ahead and bringing the story back to herself.

"We went to Thrillers? God, I can't remember shit. I think I'm still drunk." Jack looked around, "Really?"

"Yes," Layla confirmed.

Amber scowled at Larry. "We weren't there for too long," she said.

"Remember, Jack?" Layla tried to jog his memory,

"That's when you took that tequila shot for me."

"Ah, yes!" he responded.

"That's when we all decided to take the bus back to Putney."

"It was like 2:00 A.M., by then."

"I'd sobered up somewhat, y'all."

"Me, too."

"Yeah, until we got here!"

"Do you remember doing cartwheels in the backyard?" Paula looked at Jack—he looked back, blankly. Paula continued, "You don't remember when you cartwheeled into the bush?"

"I do! My Band-Aid!" He exclaimed.

"Then, Jude cut his finger on a bottle, and you guys had matching Band-Aids."

"Band-Aid buddies!" Layla and Sharon sang together.

Meanwhile, Alex made a sideways peace sign indicating he'd chosen scissors. Larry's hand was flat out, showing he'd picked paper. An expression of defeat washed over his face. Smack! Larry reeled in pain, grabbing his arm, and finally cried out, "Damn it!" A couple of pigeons flew from the tree next to the house, and some white feathers drifted down to the ground.

"That was violent," Jack commented. "Was that really six inches?"

"So, Jude cut his hand opening the bottle, and we smoked," Alex continued.

"We made quesadillas!" Sharon said.

"I made quesadillas!" Layla corrected.

"Excellent quesadillas, by the way."

"Hey, I helped," Sharon insisted.

"Oh, come on," said Layla, "You could barely talk, and you kept trying to put ketchup on them while I was cooking! I had to physically keep you away from the food so you wouldn't ruin it." All who remembered the scene laughed and agreed with Layla.

"What?" Sharon said with a guilty laugh, changing the

subject. "I didn't like how Kenny was going on about legalizing pot like it would solve all the world's problems."

"His point was just that governments shouldn't be so stubborn. They should just grant people the opportunity to try it and see if it works. I thought he made a good argument."

"That's because you're a pothead, Chestnut," said Paula.

"Then, we played Perudo."

If you've never played Perudo, it is also known as Liar's Dice. The game requires each player to start with a cup, five dice, basic arithmetic, and a poker face. There is no limit to how many people can play, as long as you have enough dice and cups. Originally an ancient South American game, it was later appropriated and beloved by pirates who helped promote it internationally. Hundreds of years later, in the 1970s, it was the first professional sport to include official drinking rules. The Golden Age of Perudo culminated with the infamous 1977 Masters of the Dice International Championship debacle. Intense public scrutiny drove away sponsors, causing the sport to fade from the mainstream.

Relative to this night of debauchery, everyone had agreed to play by the official Masters of The Dice International (MDI) rules. The rules state that if a die falls off the table and lands on the ground—known as an "off the table"—you have to take a shot of alcohol for each die you've lost.

"Perudo! Good grief, I knocked my whole cup off the table," Layla said.

"Four shots!" Paula said. Jack shook his head.

Layla sighed, "I took them,"

"They weren't full shots," Alex replied.

"The Hero came through again, and won the game," said Sharon.

Layla looked around, "I don't remember that."

"You were passed out with your head on Jack's shoulder, by then," Tristan said. Alex punched Larry in the arm. Larry squealed.

"That's when Larry and Alex started their Olympics in

the backyard. Yeah, they played like fifteen games of Perudo after Jack won," Amber said.

"What happened to…?" Jack tried to ask about the other partygoers.

"You guys were wasted." Paula interjected in frustration, "Jude and Sharon started hooking up in the library. Kenny walked in on them twice, and then they went upstairs. Audrey and Louis were inside talking. Then, Kenny tried to cook while Chloë and Amber watched. Tristan and I were on the couch, stoned out of our minds, and Jack carried Layla upstairs to put her to bed after she passed out. He came back, put out Kenny's cooking fire, and called a cab for Chloë, Audrey, and the Aussies. The taxi pulled up at sunrise. You (Jack), Larry, and Alex took a row of whiskey shots. Larry puked and we all went to sleep, except Larry, who was vomiting in the grass, and Alex, who was making fun of him."

"You know, I'd forgotten about those whiskey shots, until right now," said Jack.

"Yup, sounds right. That's when I started my ludicrous winning streak on this douchebag," Alex said, brandishing his knuckles.

"Go fuck yourself! This is supernatural," Larry exclaimed, rubbing his arm. "I feel like shit."

"That's funny, because I feel like the righteous hand of God," Alex retorted.

"The End?" Layla asked.

Not yet. Bones silently replied, as she leapt off the roof. Jack saw the vulture first but didn't have time to warn anyone. He just braced himself for someone to scream. The impending moment slowed the morning activities to a screeching halt. The pigeons began their cascading exodus from the sprawling branch of the old oak tree. The weight of Bones shook the tree limb, as she dug her claws into her new perch, twelve feet above their heads. The commotion caused a wave of feathers to cascade from the tree above and flutter softly to the ground. Jack watched them fall behind Layla—her khaki pants reminded him of his dream, like Déjà Vu.

"*Eeeeeeekk!*" Paula's scream was the loudest.

"Ah tu merde!" Tristan exclaimed.

"Holy shit, y'all!"

"Hey, look, my friend, your bird."

"Wow! That's a big buzzard!"

"Dude, this thing really is following you."

CHAPTER 26
DUSTIN, 1:56 P.M

Dustin walked a full circle around the area where he and Jack were supposed to meet. The afternoon sun warmed his skin through the cold air. He stood and sipped his coffee. Dustin wore designer blue jeans; scuffed, brown dress shoes; a tucked-in, grey collared shirt; a red, hooded sweatshirt; and a red belt. The outfit had lost a bit of luster because he'd been wearing it since the night before.

Dustin usually didn't take the time to learn someone's name, but rather decided, based on the situation, if they were a: buddy, chief, hoss, amigo, or captain. He was a polarizing character and the people who knew him either had a funny story to go along with it, or basically hated him. It was Dustin's last day in London, before returning to the studio in New York to start pre-production for *The Blob 2*.

Jack had called Dustin's cell phone from the Chapel's house in Putney, soon after the commotion with Bones. He told Dustin he had to go home, first. So, Dustin immediately acted like something was wrong, and insisted Jack come directly to Hyde Park, and that they could swing by his place before they went out later. Reluctantly, Jack agreed and said he would be there at 1:30 P.M.

It was almost two o'clock, and Jack was thirty minutes

late. Dustin was aggravated because Jack didn't have a cell phone, and he couldn't call him and tell him how annoyed he was. Dustin stared into the distance and reflected on Carrie kicking him out of her apartment. Instead of getting a hotel room, he used the money and went to an all-night strip club. He'd sobered up while at the club but by this time had started drinking again.

A skinny man with a mustache wearing a Toronto Maple Leafs windbreaker recognized Dustin from a movie. Dustin didn't notice him until the man's voice interrupted his thoughts.

"Excuse me, eh?" he said, "Aren't you the guy from those movies?" Dustin gave him a curious look. "Oh! I guess that's vague, eh. You know, like that one where Grace Jones is a rickshaw driver and you say, 'Damn, bitch! You look like a retarded Wesley Snipes with breasts and a dick.' Then, she decapitates you."

"*Blades of Blood*," Dustin casually replied.

"Yeah! It is you! I can't believe the awful shit you say in your movies. Is that why you have the First Amendment? So you can say terrible things to people?" Neither could Dustin believe the balls on this stranger, nor appreciate where the Canuck was driving with his question. He pondered before responding.

"I just read the script," Dustin said, then took a sip of coffee and looked at his watch: 2:09.

"Well, you know it before you say it on film, right? It's not like you're morally exempt from the vulgar and hateful things that come out of your mouth, eh."

"Seriously, boss? What do you want from me, an apology to Wesley Snipes? Do you want an autograph or something?"

"Nah, really, I'm okay."

Now, Dustin was glaring at him. The man took a few steps backward, then turned and continued down the pedestrian path.

Dustin noticed Jack, finally coming around the corner

past a couple of trees. He wore the same grey jacket, corduroy pants, and Converse sneakers as the night before. Jack spoke first, "You look like the Captain of a floating pile of shit. What the hell happened to you?"

"Well, Carrie broke up with me. She kicked me out."

"Why?" *He already knew.*

"I was cheating on her."

"I mean, you're just incredible," Jack showered Dustin in disapproval, "Carrie is so hot; she's funny; she's intelligent; and you go off, and you cheat on her with the sleaziest, craziest, most dimwitted, annoying, transparent sluts I've ever seen. Who was it this time? Was it some chick you found in a tattoo parlor?" Jack asked, amused with himself.

"Bridget," Dustin announced. Jack instantly stopped smiling.

"You've been having sex with my roommate?" He shouted, then calmly continued. "Well, I guess it does prove my point about your choice in women...in the apartment? When?"

"Yeah, when you go to work. Bridget gets home around six-thirty. I show up. I just tell her to take her clothes off. She does! She basically does whatever I tell her to do. It's just fine.

Carrie is a great woman, but I don't need a great lady. I need pussy. She makes me work too hard. I work for everything. If I wanted to beg for sex, I would be single, and I sure as fuck wouldn't have become a movie star. Don't hate me if I don't fall for that age-old love conspiracy. Women are allowed to lure you in with good sex and love, and the second you tell them that they're the only one for you: Boom! Suddenly, your entire sex life is based on your ability to follow their orders. You have to do what they say when they say it, or no sex! That's not love, that's fucking vaginal blackmail. It's evil!

I go out, women love me, and I'm the criminal! I'm the victim here. I was hornswoggled into monogamy to begin with. I would never have started dating her if she had mentioned we could only have sex when she wanted to, and only in a window of about three and a half minutes before she found another reason to be pissed off at me. She's not free, either. Love isn't free. Bridget wants to have sex all the time."

Dustin paused while he made a critical assessment of Jack's attire, "I look like shit? Aside from that clean shave, you look like McMasters just napalmed your village. What the hell happened to you?"

"Not much," said Jack. "I've been wearing the same clothes as yesterday, and there's this fucking vulture following me everywhere. By the way, I still haven't caught what was so important that I couldn't go home and get cleaned up first. I could probably be hanging out with Layla right now, with clean clothes on. Was it you breaking up with Carrie?"

"Huh? Oh, nothing. That was what we call acting. I figured you wouldn't see it coming, and I didn't feel like playing with myself out here for another forty-five minutes while you put on your fucking lipstick. Who's Layla?"

"Damn, you're so selfish." Jack shook his head.

"Jack-baby, shit. I'm sorry! I wanted you out here. We're a team. I'm leaving tomorrow. Is it really a crime to want to spend extra time with your best friend?"

Dustin jerked back defensively, as Bones appeared and flapped her enormous wings. She glided over their heads, then looped in a circle in the sky above.

"Holy shit! Where did that bird come from?"

"I just told you it was following me. Let's go." Jack gave Dustin a recap of Thursday and Friday as they made their way through the park. Bones soared above them. Dustin watched the bird and sipped his coffee, Jack talked, and a female jogger in high shorts rubbernecked to watch Bones as she ran by. Dustin and Jack stopped everything and checked her out.

"So, what happened after that thing landed on the tree

and scared everyone? Is that when you called me?" Dustin asked.

"Yeah. When I got back outside, Layla had arranged to leave, too. She had to catch a train to Oxford." Jack looked at his watch—it was still broken.

"What's in Oxford?"

"Her ex-boyfriend."

"Oh, no."

"I knew it was too good to be true."

"But it sounds like you were in there for a minute. Did you get some?" Dustin asked.

"For a minute, I was." Jack was nostalgic, "I guess I got a little carried away," he chuckled thinking about it, "I don't care how cool you are, man, when you fall in love, it just changes you. On the train, we watched each other through the reflection in the glass. She put her head on my shoulder, and we held hands, she commented that we were a cute couple. At Paddington station, we hugged good-bye. A minute after that, she was gone. Honestly, I've been trying not to forget the feeling of being next to her. It was like a dream come true."

"Is that it? You hugged? So, basically, you held hands with this girl. You know what? Don't tell anyone else that story. It's the most impotent thing I've ever heard! You were with all those chicks and you didn't even make out with one of them? What? Why? You're no me, but you're better than that. I'm disappointed. Are you sure this vulture isn't following me? I think it would make more sense." Jack looked at him in disbelief, but Dustin ignored him, "So are you gonna call this chick?"

"No. If I start living like she's missing from my life, then I'm taking a piece away from something that is already whole. I'm not looking for a pen-pal, either. I'm going to be thirty in a few years."

"What, no desperate-ass love poems?"

"I actually wrote one," Jack said, sarcastically, "It's a short one. You'll like it."

"Let's hear it, Emerson."

"Dustin, / it would be fun, / to see you run, / and then, jump into a woodchipper."

"Your poetry sucks."

"Yeah, anyway, the only way for me to ever restore the perfectly whole person I was before her, is just to let her go."

"What are you talking about? Whole person? You never let any of them go. How many girls have you chased to the airport in some last-minute declaration of love? I've tried to explain it to you, but you don't get it. Relationships don't start at airports. They start early in the morning with alcohol and marijuana. Plus, I've seen you drag every other girl into the next relationship like it proves something. I don't get it. Talking about past relationships to new girls is about as useful to getting laid as carrying around a festering corpse. It's a failure. Unless you're ready to truly swap stories and hear about the time a chick had anal sex with the cable repair guy, because she was feeling lonely, I suggest you stick with current affairs."

"I didn't talk about any past relationships," Jack said.

"Sure. Anyway, if you think you can do it, go for it. Just don't say all this now and start getting all down later because you want attention. I lost the love of my life last night, too." Dustin took another sip of his now lukewarm coffee.

"So, what are we doing, now?" asked Jack.

"I don't know. Wait. Yes, I do." Dustin stopped looking at the vulture and looked at Jack. "You remember in Italy, when we split up into two groups and we each found a street performer that could juggle?"

"Yeah, the scavenger hunt we made up."

"Do you remember when the teams met up in front of Andromeda and we had them juggle for that pile of lira we made?"

"Juggle, Nico! Juggle goddammit!" Jack said, as he pretended to throw money on the ground. "That was the best."

"It's not that it was the best. It is the best—don't live in the past. This bird is the here and now. Guys like us don't sit around and wait for Fun to find us. Even when times are tough, we go out, grab Fun by the balls, and punch it in the teeth; then, shake it down to make sure it's not holding out on us."

"Frankly, that doesn't sound too enjoyable for Fun," said Jack.

"That doesn't matter. The point is, this bird is an entirely unforgettable reason to have a celebration, today."

"Are you already drunk?" Jack questioned.

Dustin looked at him, shook his cup, and said, "No, but this coffee has an airplane bottle's worth of whiskey in it." He took a sip, then asked, "So, do I have to explain everything that I'm about to do, or are you just going to trust me?"

"Can I please change my clothes, first?"

"I don't even have a second pair of clothes, hombre. We'll be home in three hours. You'll be fine."

Jack looked at Dustin without answering, and then he looked up at Bones as she flew overhead, again. He missed Layla. Acknowledging he was along for the ride, Jack changed the subject and asked, "If you got to choose your last words, what would they be?"

CHAPTER 27
SPEAKER'S CORNER, 2:36 P.M.

Bones was on autopilot. Inside, Wings was relieved that Layla was out of the picture, but she—Jack's dream girl—was still locked within a vulture, and she had only eaten once in the past three days. The bird was growing steadily more desperate and weaker with each hour that passed. Wings flew low to make sure Jack could see her, watching as he and Dustin crested a hill and approached Marble Arch.

Today, Speaker's Corner was more of a long curve than a proper corner. Located at the northeast edge of Hyde Park, the area had a wide, cobblestone walking path, which created a buffer zone between the serenity of the park and the commotion of London's central business district.

The orators of Speakers' Corner shouted over one another from their pulpits made of crates, chairs, and stepstools. They formed a territorial zig-zag pattern on alternate sides of the path, about twenty meters away from one another, each one within earshot of the next. Their voices faded together into the sound of vendors barking at an outdoor market, where all that was being sold were politics, religion, and opinions. One gauged the success of a speaker by the size of the crowd watching them.

"I will put it in my will, that if I don't say, 'tell the world my story'—and nothing more—upon facing immediate death, that you are to be paid fifteen US dollars," Dustin said to Jack, as they and the bird approached a mass of onlookers.

"Agreed, but if you do win—since there will probably only be three of us at your funeral—would you want me to pay the money to the prostitute or the drunk clown?"

"It really depends on how drunk the clown is. Use your own, personal discretion."

It wasn't abnormal for this part of the park to be so congested. Historically, Saturday was the day of the week with the largest crowds. Jack and Dustin slowed their pace as they entered the mesh of human cultures and accents. Dustin was analyzing each of the speakers, looking for something that one of them might have. The pair's conversation about last words faded away.

Among the speakers was a dark-skinned man with a middle eastern accent. He was presenting his case that news organizations utilize subliminal messaging to influence and mislead the public. Across from him, was a shorter and slightly older man in a linen jacket, who wanted to create a digital system of government—without politicians—where citizens could participate in all its areas and levels, directly. He called it the Digital Democracy.

While Jack was listening, Dustin approached a man wearing blue overalls. The sun shone through his thinning hair and added beads of sweat to his brow. He was standing off to the side of the other speakers, holding a black folding chair, a tiny, white megaphone, and a newspaper.

The smell of a gyro and memories of Layla distracted Jack. He looked around for them—no lamb meat and tzatziki sauce, no Layla—he sighed.

Thirty meters ahead, Dustin had already given the middle-aged man £20 to rent his spot and equipment for a few minutes. He turned around, holding the megaphone and chair, expecting Jack to be right behind him. When he couldn't find him, Dustin spotted Jack, zoned out, and yelled his name and signaled him over.

Meanwhile, conversations about Bones had quickly spread throughout the crowd. A couple of the speakers started to capitalize on her inexplicable presence. Sensing this encroachment, Dustin suddenly stood up on the chair and held the megaphone to his lips. Bones was his phenomenon, and he didn't want some barefoot lunatic standing on a plastic crate to steal his thunder.

"This is the proof! The end is coming!" A speaker from behind the crowd exclaimed.

Dustin addressed the man's concern through the megaphone. "Sir, now that's enough of that. It's a beautiful day out, and there is no need to go scaring people. How's everybody doing today? You guys look fabulous, seriously! Especially you. I like that hat. Everyone, I'm Dustin Switch. For some of you, this is your lucky day. Let me explain…"

"Is that really Dustin Switch?" Azza said to his best mate, Dave-o, as they stood in front of the gathering crowd.

"It's hard to tell, without his bloody ridiculous mustache," replied Dave-o.

"Fucking hell, you think they're shooting a movie or something?" It was an interesting idea. Both men decided to stick around and see what Dustin had to say.

CHAPTER 28
THE PUB CRAWL, 2:43 P.M.

Seizing the moment, Dustin introduced Bones as the menacing vulture that was following him around the park. While he had their attention, he did his best impersonation of a humble movie star who was looking to give back to the wonderful people who had made him famous. His big plan was to get a bunch of random people together and start a spontaneous pub crawl, right then, and there. He wanted to march the crowd west on Wigmore Street, then south on Regents Street, towards Piccadilly Circus—where the majority of the clubs and nightlife would be found. Dustin attempted to entice the indecisive people by offering to buy the first round of drinks for everyone.

Deep down, Dustin was hoping this gimmick would translate into some sort of 1980's beer commercial fantasy; where an absurd number of beautiful women, from which to choose a mate for the evening, surrounded him.

Unfortunately for Dustin's ego, when he was finished with his speech, most of the people listening went back to what they were doing. Only fourteen members of the audience, mostly guys, decided to take him up on the offer.

The shortfall only temporarily discouraged Dustin, and he found new hope in the four South American brunettes who decided to join. He immediately began flirting with Maria, Consuela, Sofia, and Mariana. Also joining were Rory and Breezy, an American couple from the Midwest celebrating their engagement in London; two Jamaicans, Bee and Raj; two Australians, named Dave-o and Azza; Danny and Manny, a pair of gay lovers who met in college; Jack Chestnut; and the vulture.

King Henry's Tavern was the fourth bar on the road to Piccadilly. It was a long and narrow street. The service counter inside projected about five feet from the wall, and ran the length of the right side of the pub. Wood panel walls, the lacquered wood bar, sets of wooden pillars, wooden stools, and a wood floor covered with a green and red paisley carpet made it feel like they were inside a cigar box. The smoke billowed, level above the heads of the crowd—it was obvious that the ventilation was insufficient.

Dustin's idea to take a shot at the first bar transformed into taking a shot at every bar, every hour: 3:00 Red's Tavern, 4:00 The Lamb, 5:00 McFlanagen's, and it was now 5:58, at King Henry's. Everyone at the bar held their shots up in anticipation. The chime of clinking glasses rang, as everyone got ready to imbibe another round of liquor.

Jack Chestnut was almost drunk—he wasn't the only one, either. In four hours of drinking, the group of fourteen had gone from total strangers to casual acquaintances. Rory and Breezy chanted in unison, "Speech! Speech! Speech!" It was time for a toast. For Dustin, if two people wanted him to give a speech, it was two more than needed. Again, he stood on a nearby chair and spoke.

"First and foremost, I'd really like to genuinely thank myself for having this fucking great idea. Let's give it up one more time for me!" He raised his hands like a victorious boxer. The audience laughed and applauded, drunkenly. "Thank you, thank you! You're beautiful. This afternoon, when I stood on that folding chair and asked you to all join me in this adventure, you weren't scared. You didn't call your mommies and ask permission. You saw a once-in-a-lifetime opportunity to do something memorable and you took that bitch! I'm proud of all of you. Cheers."

"Shot!" everyone shouted at 6:00. They lifted their glasses, tilted their heads back, and a hundred quid of smelly tequila disappeared.

Jack's mouth burned like warm, sour acid, and for a moment, he thought of nothing but the tequila; not Layla, not Wings, not the vulture, not The Cask & Glass, not Bridget, not his family, or even his vacation to Greece. He had no thoughts of true love, his positions on politics and society, or how to articulate his quirky nuances into English to sound cool but not pretentious. Everything he had ever thought about went away and the miserable serenity of trying not to vomit wholly consumed Jack's thoughts.

The empty shots clacked against the bar, playing the same, flat note. Danny ran to the bathroom, holding his mouth; Manny went after him, carrying his partner's matching jean jacket. The Aussies returned to the bar and ordered two more shots, while they watched the last four minutes of a soccer game on the TV above their heads. Breezy and Rory began to make out near the back. Dustin was hitting on Consuela. Jack, who wasn't really talking to anyone, missed Layla again and wanted some fresh air. Raj saw Jack leave and decided to follow him outside because it seemed like a good idea. Bee followed blindly, while he typed a text message. Maria, who hadn't smoked since coming to Europe, saw an excellent opportunity to do so. She casually tailed all three men to find out if that is what they were going to do.

The taste of tequila faded from Jack's tongue as he walked outside of King Henry's, unannounced. He lit a cigarette and was greeted by the vulture, peering at him from her streetlight perch. They locked eyes for a moment, then the bird released a furious squawk of contempt and frustration when she saw he was not alone. The three others came out and joined him on the sidewalk closest to the pub. Raj began to roll a joint, Bee finished his text, and Maria approached Jack. Her English was strong, and he had no trouble understanding her.

"So, what's up dude?" she said, "Everybody here is having such a good time and you look like you just lost your puppy."

Jack watched the bird sitting on the streetlight across the road.

"Really?" he asked, without looking at her. He didn't feel like answering the question, but he didn't want to be too defensive, either.

"Is it that vulture bothering you?"

"Who? Bones? Nah."

"Is it a girl?" Jack looked at Maria, and she knew. "Is she dead?"

"I look that sad? Jesus, no, she's alive. I just don't think that I'll ever see her again."

"Poor thing, well, you probably can't change where she is. Maybe you can change where you are. Selfless decisions are an important part of love."

"Like, go to where she is going to be? I couldn't follow her to New York. It's too crazy! It's creepy."

"Obviously, I don't know the details, but think, if you're right for her, you could show up in Timbuktu, and she won't freak out. She'll just be that much happier to see you. One crazy person is psychotic, yes, but two crazy people together and in love is as cute as it gets." Maria paused. "Besides, all I'm saying is, if your heart is in the right place, and it is pleading with you to act, there's a chance that she feels the same way, too. If that is the case, then you're not going to have to convince her of anything. You won't even have to explain why you are there. If you're wrong, well, sure, it will be extremely awkward, but at least you'll have a great story to tell your buddies. Embarrassing stories are the best!" The pungent aroma of burning cannabis drifted across their conversation.

Bee interrupted, "Hey, mama, you wanna hit this?"

"For sure, Bee!" Maria said, happily. Jack felt a little

better. He stared at Bones for another minute; smiled, thinking about Layla; and went back inside.

The crawl moved to the Black Horse after the soccer match finished. Manny, Danny, and Sofia shared a cab home. 7:00. "Shot!" The crawl was at its drunken peak at the tiny Bricklayer's Arms. "Shot!" 8:00. Breezy and Rory, who had been making out for hours, left to return to their hotel room.

CHAPTER 29
DRUNK, 9:22 P.M.

Outside Fitzroy Tavern, from a nearby tree, the vulture tried to catch a glimpse of Jack through the large, arched red windows. The exaggerated proportions of the booth made Dustin, Jack and everyone else—Bee, Raj, Dave-o, Azza, and Harry—look like children. The three girls were in line for the bathroom. The pace of drinking had slowed down, and everyone was showing signs of inebriation. Bones wasn't sure if she was dying of starvation or a broken heart, but pain consumed her weakened body.

Inside, Dustin naturally became the center of attention, and he loved it. Since multiple people were talking to him at once, he tried to answer everyone's questions in the order they were asked, "Bee, I get the chutzpa from my father...not that I ever met the piece of shit. All I know, is he was the first Jew to own a used Volkswagen dealership after the war; fucking scum of the earth. I channel his dead, worthless soul every time I try to take it to the next level of insensitive douchebaggery."

"Is that why you grow a mustache?"

"Yes." Dustin responded, absolutely, then continued, "Azza, I don't live long in my movies, but I charge a lot. I'm basically an icon. Thirty minutes is the longest I've ever lived: *The Legend of Dachshund Island*, where the porn stars are shipwrecked on an island infested with man-eating dachshunds."

"Oh God, those dachshunds tore you apart!"

"That was classic! Didn't Repici direct that, too?" Dave-o asked. Dustin nodded to Dave-o, then noticed that Jack was dismayed. In fact, he was in a distant, disinterested, and distracted state. Dustin needed to cheer him up.

"Jack, dude, lighten up, little homie. You have a lot less than me, but you still have tons of things to celebrate and be happy for. Stop focusing on Nikki; it's out of your hands."

"Nikki?" Jack looked around befuddled, "Who the fuck is Nikki? Her name is Layla, jerk-off. And why are we talking about it? I wasn't making a big deal about it."

"You're wearing it on your face."

"So! You don't understand. I'm pretty sure I just took a once-in-a-lifetime, supernatural event—catered to me—and flushed it down the toilet. You don't just let that go. I'll think about what I could have done differently for the rest of my life."

"So? What the fuck are you going to do, now? Chase after her, like that girl you met in Italy? So you can replace her fading memory of you as a nice guy with the overwhelming evidence that you're a desperate schmuck? Are you writing a sequel to that lame poetry book, "The Ocean of Self Pity?""

"It's called *The Song of Her Sea*," Jack dryly corrected Dustin.

"It doesn't matter. Nobody's read it. Correction: I've read it, and your mom's read it, and that's not a mom joke. Regardless, the only thing supernatural is that freaking vulture outside. I don't care if it's from the zoo. You shouldn't have fed the thing, and you should call the fucking Animal Control office. Stop diluting reality from what it is, to what you want it to be. Every time you get a hard-on, you start acting like you're a character in a romance novel; then

116

when you realize you're not—you're just normal—then, we get this guy." Dustin made an exaggerated sad face, "No credits are waiting to roll on your own happy ending, hoss. I know you've had some setbacks, but you're good. What about that ancient guy with the beard, over there at the bar? Does it look like he got his happy ending? You think some kid who steps on a landmine playing soccer has a happy ending? Shit. In life, happiness is the exception; misery is what's guaranteed. Yes, I get it. For a minute, she might have thought of kissing you, but by tomorrow, she's going to be fucking her ex-boyfriend, or some other guy, just because he created an opportunity, then got the job done." Dustin ended on that point, but before Jack could respond, everyone else at the table added their own opinions to the discussion.

"He's got a point, mate," Azza replied.

"One person in love doesn't hack it," Raj said.

"Son," Harry said, "Love is like life. At first, you're looking down from the top of a giant, spiral carnival slide and you can't see how far it goes, but it looks like more fun than you can even imagine. In fact, at that moment, it looks like so much fun that before you realize that there is no turning back, you've already jumped on the slide and it's too late. You instantly realize you haven't thought the decision through, because your shorts are too short and the sweat from your thighs is dragging you to a screeching, flesh-rending halt every few meters. You eventually give up on trying to slide. You resign to scooting yourself all the way down, while everyone else flies past you. Finally, when you get to the bottom, there is a sign that reads, "Congratulations, you're dead! Sorry, but there is no such thing as heaven. How was the ride?" That's not the worst part. When I was…"

"Harry?" Jack jumped in, "You have more to add? I just met you ten minutes ago, buddy. I don't want to hear the "worst" part. The stuff before it was depressing enough. Everyone, I understand that love and life may be more difficult over time, but that makes the selection of those you spend your life with that much more important." Jack looked at Dustin, Azza, Bee, Dave-o, and Raj, "I understand it takes two people to be in love. It has to start somewhere. I refuse to believe all relationships begin with some form of alcohol or drug-fueled sexual encounter. Can't two people just recognize and acknowledge they love each other and move forward like rational adults?"

"Oh, my god!" Dustin interjected, "You fucking said 'love' three times! The point is that "term" is not applicable in this situation. You didn't have a relationship! You hung out for a night."

The girls returned to the table and all the guys except Jack instantly turned their attention to them. Dave-o stood up, but never sat back down. He and Maria began to make-out by the jukebox, then disappeared. Dustin, not wanting to be upstaged by the Aussie, unsuccessfully attempted to persuade Consuela and Mariana into a threesome, resulting in them getting creeped out and leaving immediately.

"Shot!" It was 10:00 P.M., at The Ben Crouch Tavern. Bee and Raj had followed Dustin, Jack, and Azza, but when they realized that all the girls were gone and that they weren't coming back, the two decided to go elsewhere to look for women.

"Shot!" Dustin shouted at the Bradley's barman at 11:00. Jack had his head down and his shot glass in the air. Azza held two shot glasses and looked the bartender dead in the eyes; he was in high spirits. The barmen handed Dustin his change and said, "Take your shots, and get the fuck out of me pub."

PART IV:
SUNDAY, AUGUST 15TH, 2006

CHAPTER 30
CLUB MONDO, 12:00 A.M.

Inside Club Mondo, Dustin, Azza, and Jack took their ninth shot in as many hours and dispersed to see what the establishment had to offer. Thirty minutes later, Dustin and Jack were near the back bar and service exit. Jack was hunched over at a nearby table staring at his wrist, trying to make out the time on his broken watch. He could only get his eyes to focus for a matter of milliseconds. He was exhausted. The music was so loud that he could feel the sound bouncing off the hairs of his skin. The lights flickered in patterns with the rhythm.

Dustin was at the bar, waiting for his drinks and looking for available women. He watched three girls on the lip of the dance floor, then turned around and lost his smile when he saw the bartender sensibly limiting the alcohol in the cocktails that he'd ordered. Multitasking the order, the barman placed them in a line with some other drinks in the cocktail taxiway.

"That fucking cunt," Dustin said, inaudible against the

sea of pounding dance music, then moved over to Jack. He wanted to talk to the ladies, and he wanted Jack's help. The music was only slightly dimmed towards the back of the club and there was no way to talk without yelling. Dustin leaned over and yelled to Jack, "That greasy piece of shit bartender poured us half-shots."

"Huh?" Jack shouted.

"I may be rich, but I'm not a schmuck."

"What are you talking about?"

"The bartender! Jesus, Jack, straighten up." Jack stood up straight, then slouched again, shortly after that. Dustin continued, "The bartender barely put any booze in our drinks!"

"Then don't tip him, if you want to be a dick." The drinks arrived shortly. Dustin gave a phony smile and asked for the tab.

He brought the drinks over. "*If I want to be a prick?*" he said. "I get paid to make people hate me. I have a professional obligation to my fan base to react to this situation appropriately and proportionally."

The bartender signaled that he had the check. Dustin went to the bar and defiantly grabbed the pen. He wrote an enormous, bold zero across the dotted tip line and signed the bill "Fuck You."

Meanwhile, Jack was out of regular cigarettes and cash. He began to hand-roll a cigarette from a pouch that Dave-o had left. It was sloppy, and tobacco was raining on the floor. Jack's motor skills were suffering. His fingers were stiff, and he looked like a gorilla trying to use chopsticks. He missed Layla.

Dustin returned, "You see those three girls, next to the sweaty dude in the polka-dot rayon shirt?" He yelled.

Jack didn't look up, "The brunette and the blonde are cute, but the one with curly hair is a little rough."

"Yeah, what do you think that is on the side of her face? Like, an infection or something?"

"I'm not sure; it could be a massive birthmark. I've seen

that before."

Dustin countered, "We're running out of time. Can you handle a reverse to the weak-side?" He asked, referencing a thoroughly dissected night of debauchery from a couple years earlier. Jack immediately knew his plan.

"No, you are drunk. I'm going middle. And I'm not doing weak-side with two people; you need three."

"Azza!" Dustin said, both addressing and looking past Jack.

"Fucking hell. Is Azza still here?"

"I see him, right now. He's walking over. It's quantity over quality for those salty pirates. I doubt he'll have any apprehension." Azza shuffled between a few people as he approached with half a bottle of Fosters in his hand.

"Hey you, fuckwits! All they had was this bloody Foster's piss. I fuckin' hate Foster's."

"Great, Azza! We need your help!" This statement peaked Azza's interest, sensing a scheme. The men turned their backs to the dance floor to dampen the sound, but Dustin still had to shout, "First, Jack is going to walk up to these three chicks. He's polite and witty, and shit. He is magnificent with making strange girls feel comfortable, getting their names, and making them all feel pretty." Dustin looked at Jack—he shrugged his shoulders. "And then, I am going to show up with a little charisma and panache. If they don't recognize me, Jack will introduce us. Then, you come in and start hitting on to the girl that's starting to feel left out. This way, everyone is happy."

"You slimy sepo cunt! I want you to know that I know exactly why you need my help, and I'm perfectly okay with it."

"Exactly, my friend!"

"You ready, Jack?" Azza asked, doubtfully.

"I'm down." Jack felt a wave of sobriety.

"Showtime, Jack."

They turned to face the three bouncers standing shoulder-to-shoulder, each one was slightly smaller than the next, like a set of grisly babushka dolls with English accents. The middle-sized one in the center waved Dustin's receipt, then said, "Hey! Which one of you Yank cunts wrote this?"

"Fuck off, I'm from Australia!" Azza said.

CHAPTER 31
BROKE, 12:16 A.M.

Everyone stepped back for a second, before things escalated too quickly, to see if there was a misunderstanding. Dustin took the lead and the receipt from the bouncer to inspect it. He verified it had a £0 tip and "Fuck You" written on the signature line. He discreetly put the receipt in his pocket, as he tried to explain that Jack and Azza really had nothing to do with his actions, and that they should be allowed to stay.

Jack standing nearest to the table, listening as best he could while slightly wobbling. He was trying to hand-roll another cigarette. His gin and tonic was next to him. His small wave of sobricty had crested and dipped back down into total drunkenness. Azza had no idea what was going on, but anxiously gripped his Foster's bottle.

The shortest of the bouncers watched Jack trying to roll a cigarette and decided that he, in particular, needed to go. To everyone's surprise, Jack, sensing the bouncer's intentions, nimbly took his drink from the table, and stepped backward, avoiding the security guard's sluggish lunge. The dodge knocked all the tobacco out of his cigarette paper and onto the floor. Jack was disappointed in the loss, but quickly pushed it to the back of his mind. He confidently pointed his index and middle finger at the bouncer, while nesting the glass in his other fingers.

"Fuck you," he said, "This is bullshit. You know I didn't do anything. Go ahead and kick me out if you need to, but you're not getting this drink! It's paid for." Jack bravely took the last gulp, held the glass out like he was surrendering a weapon, and let it drop to the floor.

The glass fell straight down but didn't break. There was a shared, temporary wonderment when the glass landed perfectly upright on the ground, as if it had defied physics. Jack, Azza, Dustin, and the middle bouncer watched as the largest bouncer bent down and picked up the cup of ice and salivary remnants, then set it on the table. The smallest bouncer grabbed Jack with two, big handfuls of his shirt, lifted him up and carried him like a ballistic shield, using his back to engage the opening bar on both sets of exit doors leading to the street.

In a flash backward, Jack was suddenly outside. Bones watched the commotion from across the street, then squawked at Jack. It was the second place that he'd been kicked out of that evening, and he was starting to feel ashamed of himself. It was warm and dark outside. He watched Bones and thought of Layla. Even though he knew that Dustin and Azza would surely be out in a moment, he felt utterly alone. Wings felt a similar emptiness as she watched him from her bird eyes, wishing she were still dead.

CHAPTER 32
THE TOOTH, 12:18 A.M.

Still inside, Dustin and Azza backed towards the exit. During this time, Azza broke the empty Foster's bottle over his own head, which is Australian for '*I am frustrated. Don't mess with me.*' Dustin held the exit door for Azza as he threw the broken bottle into the trashcan and left, passing the bouncer who had just kicked out Jack. They regrouped outside. While he shook bits of glass from his short, curly, blonde hair, Azza suggested they continue the pub crawl to a nearby club.

Dustin felt the receipts in his pockets and held them up proudly. Jack was too drunk to understand why he was so delighted over the pieces of paper. As the three men walked south towards the next bar, Dustin explained the situation. Since he had both copies of the receipt, Club Mondo wouldn't be able to charge his credit card. The whole stunt had landed them all free drinks.

"Very tidy, my friend!" said Azza, as they walked to the door of The Spoon. "Very tidy, indeed."

"Did you just get me thrown out of a club to save £35?" Jack asked, bewildered.

"I told you fuckwits it was close." Azza interrupted, "I'll be at the downstairs bar. The club is upstairs, in the back.

It's not that big, but there are always a hand-full of sheilas up there. I'll check it out, later."

Azza walked over to see an old friend and announced his arrival by yelling his current favorite catchphrase, "Big Time!" like Santa Claus hollering from his sleigh.

Jack and Dustin decided to remain upstairs, once they got there and ordered a couple of Red Bull and vodkas. Jack, feeling momentarily responsible, ordered an additional glass of water for himself. He thought about Putney—how Layla stood there, and he watched the feathers fall around her, like Wings in his dream. He was drunk and dejected. Dustin started a conversation with the bartender. Jack drank the water, picked his cocktail up, then staggered to the bathroom.

In the water closet, Jack used the stall, then washed his hands and face. His reflection was substantially blurrier than he was used to, but then, he felt another wave of sobriety. He was going to pull it together and make something happen. He lit a cigarette and carried it and his cocktail in his right hand, like a Frank Sinatra poster he had seen. He gathered himself and prepared to strut back to his seat. Unfortunately, after leaving the bathroom, Jack's false sense of temperance quickly faded.

Dustin was prepared to tell Jack that he looked like he was trying to walk across a canoe—but he didn't have the chance. Jack was ten meters away, deep in an internal situational monologue.

Twelve o'clock! Twenty feet and closing! Smoking hot blonde, red dress, 5'9 in heels, big C, nice waistline! I repeat: nice waistline.

Eye contact?

Confirmed.

Is she smiling back?

Roger that.

Prepare to engage the target.

Jack Chestnut knew this wasn't going to be easy. He could still talk, but he would have to improvise and avoid too much movement until he was sober enough to properly use his legs. He attempted to find a little piece of real estate near the bar to lean on, preferably somewhere sturdy where he could get comfortable. She was getting closer. Jack continued to talk to himself.

Eight feet and closing!

I can barely fucking walk. What am I posting up on?

Trashcan: left side, two feet, stay cool, keep the eye contact. Get ready to say something cute. You got this!

Jack's timing was going to be perfect and so was she— hotter than habanero peppers in a sauna. Their heads turned as they locked eyes.

Jack felt clutch. He had gotten his left hand to the rim of a plastic, rectangular trash can, and placed the burden of his weight on it before this dame could get a good look at his inability to stand upright without the assistance of a fixture. A small, plastic trashcan is certainly not a fixture.

The bin folded in, and down! Jack, lacking motor skills and a third arm, pulled the waist-high trash can on top of himself as he took a free, face-first dive into the thinning, liquor-soaked carpet. His conversation with the floor ended with him breaking the temporary cap off his right, front tooth. For a second, he swam—toothless and dazed—in the rubbish from the can.

Half of Jack's tooth, his cigarette, his cocktail, and his confidence were all lost. They were replaced with shame, a lisp, and the smell of beer, orange juice, cigarette butts, and nacho cheese. He had destroyed his nicest jacket.

Probability of getting laid: zero. I repeat: zero. System shutting down. Jack thought, finishing his inner monologue before his ego vanished, as he faced the humiliation of reality. Sensing a low point, Jack knew it was time to go home. As he was getting to his feet, he saw the bouncer coming over to kick him out. He had never been kicked out of three bars in one night. At this, he felt additionally disgraced.

"Thuck," he said, immediately realizing that a Sylvester the Cat-like lisp had replaced his mild southern drawl. Jack was now in flight-mode. He made his way to the exit, narrowly avoiding the bouncer. He never looked back to see if Dustin was coming or if anyone was watching—they were.

CHAPTER 33
THE LEG, 12:40 A.M.

There was a French couple already outside when Jack exited The Spoon. The man was on the phone with his friend and ended up describing what he saw. Fortunately, Jack never understood what he was saying.

"I'm watching this massive vulture sleeping on top of a streetlight, and this American fuck just came out of The Spoon. He's the least-sober man I've ever seen in my life. He doesn't even notice there's a vulture above him on the lamp pole. Oh my god, it just shit on him! This is incredible! It's all over this asshole's jacket. Too funny! I think he's on drugs or something. You know, he looks filthy and he's missing a tooth or two..."

The French couple snickered at Jack as he grabbed a piece of trash and tried to clean off his jacket. Dustin, who had grabbed Azza on his way out, emerged from the entrance of the pub, laughing hard about Jack's face plant. They laughed even harder when they saw the bird shit on his jacket. Azza fell to the ground. For theatrical effect, Dustin walked back inside, and then came back out the door to start laughing all over again, with Azza, who also found Dustin's gag amusing.

"Thank god it wasn't me, this time!" Dustin said, when he caught his breath. "Are you okay, chief?"

"I'm thine."

Azza and Dustin hadn't heard his lisp yet. They both burst into laughter, again.

"Thufferin' thuccotash!" Dustin exclaimed.

Jack was feeling even worse. After they'd been laughing at him for some time, he said calmly, "Lithen guyth. I had a great thime thonighth, but I'm done. If we're going thogether, then letth get a cab to Beluthi'th, tho I can get the buth from there or…"

"What!? You're not going home. It's 12:40," Dustin protested.

Jack looked frustrated, but fought it back, "I'm noth even going to acknowledgthe how sthocked I am that you exthpect me to keep drinking." He took a breath, "I love you. You're my brover. Today wath fucking cool. Unfortunately, I broke my fake thoof and I got nofing lefth in me. We can add another chapther of thith ham afther your nexth film, but I'm tho drunk and emothional right now, that I'm liable to do anyfing. I'm on the edge. Jutht help me get mythelf home."

"Doesn't Jack sound like a little hoe, right now?" Dustin asked Azza. Anger instantly consumed Jack. *Am I drunk enough to get in a fight right now?* He wondered. The answer to this question was a mighty "pimp slap" to Dustin's smug grin that left him in a temporary state of paralysis and knocked him back a step. Dustin glared at Jack.

"Damn, motherfucker! That fucking hurt!" Dustin shouted, as the shock fermented. He replayed the event in his mind. *Maybe I deserved that, but that took balls.* He angrily approached Jack, "But if you ever!" Jack, now full of adrenaline, didn't like the tone of his voice.

Smack! Jack's hand flew from his hip like a six shooter to deliver a second pimp slap.

"*Ohooo!*" Azza and the French couple said, as everyone recoiled.

Dustin took the inebriated Jack by the shoulders and pushed him backward and onto the ground, so they could have a moment to think.

Jack wasn't sure what to do next, either. He didn't want to hurt Dustin too much, and most of what he knew about fighting came from action movies and professional wrestling. *What would Goldberg do in this situation?* Jack thought. He began his staggering charge towards the waiting Dustin. Jack's dramatic thrust was clumsy, slow, and he realized he was going to get punched in the face several steps before it happened. Dustin's right fist landed in the middle of Jack's forehead, causing a tremendous change in Jack's uneasy momentum.

His ankle rolled and snapped. He immediately leapt onto his good ankle to relieve the intense pain, launching himself into the thrust of Dustin's punch. All present, including Jack, had never seen a man hurled three meters backward through the air from a single punch. Dustin felt like Hercules. Jack felt weightless until he hit the ground and slid a couple more inches. Then, he farted.

"Thtick a fork in me!" Jack yelped. Azza and Dustin, unharmed in the fight, came over to help him up. A cab stopped and honked. Trying to figure out what they had just seen, the group of onlookers unapologetically stared at the three men as they got into the cab. Bones took flight.

CHAPTER 34
THE TAXI, 12:50 A.M.

In the cab back to Belushi's, where Azza worked, Jack tried to explain that his leg was broken. Dustin's and Azza's shared counterpoint was that Jack was a natural weakling, and it would probably be fine. Then, Dustin and Jack tried to have a serious conversation about their friendship. However, they were both drunk and emotional, plus Jack had a lisp, so the whole conversation sounded like gibberish. Azza stated that the whole thing was a byproduct of typical light-weight American behavior, which Dustin and Jack both took personally and stopped talking. Outside of the cab driver's irritating pop-music playing softly from the speakers, it was quiet. Jack took in the beauty outside, consumed with thoughts of self-pity.

At Belushi's, Azza went inside straightaway to see who was there, and Dustin paid the driver. Jack waited on the sidewalk, crippled.

After the driver had left, Dustin and Jack looked at each other for a moment, both taking a mental inventory of the night, pondering where it would fit in among the various debaucheries of their friendship. Between the Vulture and Jack losing a tooth, it was sure to be memorable.

"Thorry I…thlapped you the thecondth thime," said

Jack.

"No worries. I don't really regret anything I did or said, but I hope your leg gets better."

Azza came out of Belushi's and shouted at Dustin to hurry up. Dustin and Jack gave each other a hug, parting ways. Dustin started feeling guilty that Jack was going to take a bus home, so he went ahead and gave him £10 for a cab.

For Jack, his final bad decision of the day came when he used the money for a taxi to buy a pack of cigarettes. By way of Catholic indignation, he gave the change to a homeless person outside the convenience store and began to slog his leg to the bus stop.

CHAPTER 35
A COLD DAY IN HEAVEN, 2:00 A.M.

It was early in the morning, and snowing—which was odd for the time of year—but Jack didn't mind. His leg was feeling better as he approached the front door of his apartment. He didn't remember taking the stairs up. He was just happy to be home and alive. When he opened his front door, though, it wasn't his apartment.

Jack was suddenly an invisible spectator of the last Christmas Eve that his whole family had spent together at his aunt Theta's house, in upstate New York. The heavy snow had come earlier that year, and a layer of white fluff covered everything. To Jack, it looked like a giant cloud was taking a nap on the entire town.

Carol and Theta's dad, Walter, had built the house with the help of their cousins. It was a sentimental spot for all the Chestnuts—a place of retreat.

Theta's best friend and roommate was Mary Drummond. After Carol and Lenard moved to Florida, Mary's daughter, Nathalie; her husband, Ian; and their two-year-old daughter, Michaela; moved in together. The place was a natural home, and they all celebrated the holiday as one family.

The time was dusk. Classic jazz was playing, but nobody listened to the music. Inside, the round dining room table had been recently cleared from dinner. Everyone was laughing for one reason or another.

Theta told a story about how her dentist had refused to pull her tooth because of her high blood pressure, and Ian jumped in to finish the story for her.

"...It's the third time with the same bloody toothache, and you're telling me you can't pull it because of high blood pressure!? This isn't the Poconos, Doc. This is New York City, in a crowded dentist's office. Of course, my blood pressure is going to be high."

The men laughed. Carol and Nathalie gave their sympathy to Theta, and she accepted it. Jack's sister, CC, was practicing ballet twirls in the kitchen, which was separated from the living room by a Franklin stove and a counter. Young Jack looked at little Michaela as she bounced up and down, watching CC spin. Nathalie picked the next topic, which was a conversation about how cute Jack and Michaela were. Nathalie started by commenting that they had similar eyes. Carol remarked on how beautiful Michaela was. Nathalie blushed with pride and thanked her for the compliment. Lenard got up and went out the back door to smoke. Jack watched him leave. When his mom started talking to him, he adjusted his attention to her.

"Jack, this girl is going to be a knockout, someday," Carol said, "You should stay in touch with her."

"Mom, she's two. I'm almost six! I'm starting the first grade, soon. It'd never work. Our lives are going to be too different." Jack heard the raising awe in the women's voices.

"Oh, my, Theta! Did you just hear what Jack said?"

"It was the cutest thing ever!"

No one ever took Jack seriously when he was six—it disgusted him. He felt like the center of attention. He started to get anxious, "May I be excused, please?" Jack asked.

"Oh, he is so polite, too," Natalie said.

"I know," Carol said.

"It's so adorable."

"He gets so embarrassed when you start talking about him." Jack anxiously awaited a response to his question.

"Yes, Jack, but just for a second. We're going to play a game. It's fun. It's called Perudo."

"Okay." Young Jack put his coat and hat on and followed his dad, who had stepped outside. The snowfall was silent, and the light

was almost gone from the sky. Lenard studied an oak tree.

"Hey, Jack!"

"Hey, Dad."

"Great work on the snowman, today."

"Thanks, Dad."

"I was just thinking about something my father once told me. Do you want to hear it?"

"Okay."

Before his dad could gather his thoughts, the back door opened, and CC's blonde head poked out. "Mom says to come inside. We are going to play a game!"

"What are you, her henchwoman?"

"She also said if you're smoking pot, she is going to kick your ass."

Lenard commented, scruffily, under his breath, "I can't believe my own daughter is speaking to me like this," then, spoke up, "I thought we used to be friends, CC! Come on, Jack, let's go inside. I'll tell you, later."

Jack watched his younger self, father, and sister all go inside.

He was alone. He remembered that his dad never told him what he was going to say that night. The porch light was shining through the silent darkness and white snow.

"Layla! I mean, Wings…?" He called out, trying to summon her, then heard himself. "Holy shit, you're pathetic," he said aloud. He was overwhelmed with self-pity. The door opened. It was his Dad, and he addressed Jack, directly.

"Layla? Wings!? Son, do us a favor. Shut up and listen. Stop acting like you're a damn Disney princess. You're charming, Jack, but you're standing on a mountain of bullshit. Your brother can eat, like, sixty hot dogs in five minutes *and* he has a full-time job. That's the real deal. Stop obsessing about finding the girl of your dreams. Worry about finding yourself a goal and making that the reality. Do that, and girls will come, naturally. Look at you. Your credit is a mess, you smoke too much, you are an alcoholic, you don't exercise enough, your diet is unhealthy, and you have bad posture. Unless you're looking for sympathy, these girls you keep falling in love with are out of your league. You wanna be loved? Act like you're worth it and get to work or lower your damn standards. Stop being a superficial prick. There are plenty of underachievers, like yourself, who are perfectly happy. You want the girl of your dreams? Why do you think that vulture is following you around? You need to wake up."

CHAPTER 36
A GHOST IN MOURNING, 5:45 A.M.

This was nothing like heaven and the magical times she and Jack had shared together. Flying came naturally to Wings, but that was about it. Her powerful, human emotions were too strong for Bones the vulture, diverting the bird's instincts and driving her down the path of self-destruction.

In the lightless morning, Wings could see her memories more clearly than the ground beneath her. It had been so long since she had actually been alive, that the sensations were overwhelming. The air burned the nostrils of her beak and the dry hunger churned inside her. She was isolated, brokenhearted, and terrified of dying. How did she get here? Wings couldn't remember her last life—it was only flickers. She couldn't even remember her name, or what her parents called her. She was just a little girl, who hadn't had a chance to figure out how horrific the real world could be. She was happy, loved, giggling, sick, and then, dead.

An early morning taxi drove by, casting two beams like twin lighthouses, as is careened around a corner near the park. The vulture caught a glimpse of Jack as the taxi passed by the field: laying near a couple of trees, his body was face-down, partially sprawled, and dirt and grass stains soiled his clothes.

Wings had followed his cab to Belushi's, where he said good-bye to his friend, Dustin. Several minutes and only about a hundred meters after the convenience store, it appeared that the wheels had fallen off Jack completely, and the only thing guiding him was the will to live and instinctual triangulations. Trying to maintain his balance was a struggle. Jack staggered like a zombie from one edge of the sidewalk to the other, mopping his broken leg in a zig-zag pattern to the bus stop. While waiting for his ride, he passed out on the green and black, painted bench. When the red, double-decker arrived, he frantically searched his pockets and pulled out one wrinkled note, boarded the bus, then immediately passed out. Jack missed his normal stop, then woke up about a kilometer down the road. He stumbled out of the bus, hopped a few feet, and fell down on his hands and knees. He fumbled around to get up, grabbed his leg and shouted, "Thuck!" After a moment of squirming, he looked around, completely confused—lost. Next, Jack appeared to intentionally enter the park, where he proceeded to urinate on a tree, drag his leg to a spot on a worn playing field, and pass out.

Wings watched as the black night slowly changed color. First, it turned violet, then periwinkle, then blue, and baby blue. She felt the first rays of the sun on her back. Her feathers tingled as she cut across the wind. There was dew on the grass and the top layer of dirt was moist and dark brown. She had been circling Jack's crippled body for three hours. She was exhausted, but her thoughts were ceaseless.

There was nowhere else to go, no more dreams to play in. She was a princess in an imaginary world, but not here. Where it mattered, she was imprisoned within a hideous beast. Furthermore, she had never known what it was like to be something ugly. She felt the deep cuts of rejection and isolation. It was so inconceivably cruel. Regardless of how she had gotten into the situation, she was losing faith in a romantic solution. She was losing faith in Jack—in the whole idea of being alive. She should have let him go, the second she sensed his hesitation. They would not be able to laugh about this, later. This situation was terminal, and she didn't see how that could change.

How could their dreams together be so good, and reality such a nightmare? It didn't make any sense. It was the first time they had truly been alone together. This was supposed to be their moment.

Her mood swung as she thought about ruining Jack's favorite coat. It wasn't *her* fault that he was plastered and falling into things. In fact, observing him in the real world had been a sad, informative experience. He wasn't some charismatic knight in shining armor. Jack was outstandingly average. More accurately, he was just a sad, little, insecure man, who didn't know his limits. In many ways, this whole mess was his fault—not just being trapped in the stupid bird, but all the wasted years. Wings questioned whether Jack loved her at all. She wondered if, for all that time, she had been nothing more than a nursemaid for some guy who couldn't hack it in his real life. The pain throbbed inside her, and for the first time, she felt hatred for the disgusting heap below—an embarrassment, disgracefully unconscious, all of his flaws exposed in the light of the morning.

CHAPTER 37
IN THE SHADOW OF A VULTURE,
6:05 A.M.

On a paddock of grass, the once adorable Jack Chestnut laid drunk, dirty, with half his right, front tooth missing, and a fractured ankle. He recovered consciousness slowly, like a computer booting up. Above, the vulture flew in circles around his broken body. She provided moments of cool relief from the early morning sun.

Hot, hot, hot, cold. Jack Chestnut was aware of the temperature. He felt it change in waves. His tongue investigated the inside of his dry mouth. He was missing the bottom half of his right, front tooth. *Ouch!* His right ankle wracked him with pain. He wasn't sure where he was, besides laying on the ground. He also sensed that it was morning. He inched his fingers into his pocket: he had his essentials. *Hot, hot, hot, cold.* His eyelids pulled back and he stared at the undercarriage of Bones flying above him. He felt doomed. Everyone thought he was a hero, yesterday. Now, look at him. He started to recognize the sound of the nearby traffic and it reassured him that he wasn't too far from the road. He stopped panicking.

As he sat up on his elbows, the bird swooped down and

eclipsed him—her tail feathers nearly grazing his face. Jack jerked back, like a batter dodging a high curveball, and hit the ground.

The movement caused a surge of pain in his leg. The vulture parachuted her wings to a stop three meters from Jack's feet. He didn't know if he had the strength to stand up. He tried to stay calm, but the idea of the bird pecking at him started to get the best of his mind. The vulture began to move closer—her skin, beak, and eyes, moving in locomotion with her gangly body.

Jack gave a feeble warning kick at her with his left leg. The vulture hissed and opened her wings. Jack winced in pain again from the reverberations on his broken ankle. He took a mental note to stop moving the broken leg around.

Jack moved a rubber band into a slingshot around his fingers and grabbed a nearby pebble from the dirt. He cocked it quickly and released. The small stone whipped through the air and crashed into the bird's left shoulder. A couple of her feathers popped off and fluttered through the air.

Bones let out a shrill scream and rotated away, flailing her wounded wing. Jack felt terrible for a moment, but reminded himself that, sadly, he was ripe for the picking and it was self-defense. He scrambled anxiously to get out of the situation, fearing the bird would recover soon and attack him. He grabbed his book and jacket off the ground, got on one knee and then hoisted himself up using his good leg. Now that he could see the street, he was fairly disappointed in himself for being such a coward. The bird was still nursing her wound. Jack gave his coat a brush, saw the shit stain, gagged, and decided to throw it out later—but for the moment, he would just carry the thing under his arm. He slapped the dust off his pants and adjusted his belt. He started dragging his leg towards traffic. As mentioned earlier, he kept a toothpick, hand wipe, and piece of gum in his wallet for emergencies, and this situation certainly counted. Jack used the toothpick to clean the dirt out from under his fingernails, and the wet nap to clean his face and hands. He chewed the gum to freshen his breath, and then formed it into a faux tooth, which, initially, seemed like a brilliant idea.

Jack emerged from the bushes of Regents Park at the corner of Ulster Place and Park Square West. He dragged his leg to a nearby lamppost and leaned against the pole to support his weight. A woman approached, walking her dachshund.

"I beg your pardon, mith," Jack's fake tooth made out of gum was promptly dislodged, but he continued, "Would you be tho kind ath to tell me if there wath a hothpital in the vithinity?"

"Oh my, yes, dear! Is everything alright?"

"Quithe alrighth," he smiled as she surveyed him, "and the hothpital?"

"Yes, dear, it's but a block or three South. You should see the sign. It's a great, big place."

"Thank you tho mucth."

"Well, you're very welcome, young man." Her dog began to bark and pull at the leash. "Speedy! Stop it, stop it, I say."

The wounded vulture emerged from the bushes. Jack forced himself to start dragging his leg as he had the night before, and it hurt. He took his gum out and placed it behind his ear, then removed a cigarette from the crumpled pack and started smoking. The bird stalked after him, also on foot.

Jack felt like he was in a Norman Rockwell painting, as he dragged his broken leg, racing the wounded vulture to the hospital. There were not very many people on the street, but the ones who were there looked at Jack with amusement. Some thought it was a TV show. This was all well and good for the first half of his struggle to the emergency room, but he was exhausted and severely dehydrated.

It started to hurt his feelings that no one had tried to help him, yet. It was a very lonely feeling. He blocked it out and smoked his cigarette. It seemed like Layla was the only good thing left to think about, and even that was depressing.

"Hey, mate, do you need a hand?" A man asked. Jack was so self-consumed that it took him a second to realize the guy was even talking to him. He looked at his leg, the vulture, and then back up at the gentleman.

"Thankth, I'm going to take you up on thath." Jack threw his arm over the man's shoulder, and they introduced themselves. When they arrived at the Emergency Room, Steve went forward to get a wheelchair for Jack.

Bones took flight again and perched above the hospital awning to wait for him. Wings' depression swelled inside the vulture. *Why did Jack hit me? I was just trying to help! This couldn't really be the man I loved.* She could see it now, it was just her fantasy of him—a beautiful lie that would never come true, because it was never real. He wasn't some dream world Romeo; he was an underachiever with substance abuse issues. Her thoughts grew dark as she began to court her death.

CHAPTER 38
THE HOSPITAL, 6:29 A.M.

Everything that Jack knew about socialized medicine, he learned after his arrival at the hospital that morning. He was informed that he didn't have to pay anything for the hospital visit and he was automatically registered for worker's compensation. Social Services would also contact his work for him and begin directly depositing disability payments into his bank account while he recovered. Essentially, the breaking of his leg had gotten him a paid vacation. It was easy for him to quickly make peace with the incident.

He was glad that he had brought a book, too. The first hour was spent in registration, next were the X-rays. Finally, a nurse cleaned his leg and prepared a cast for him. He was sized for his new tooth, and then it was attached and finished. Jack also gained some new accessories; namely, a beige wristband and a blue cast, with matching, blue and silver crutches. The color scheme made him feel sporty—though he knew he was the exact opposite.

Jack wasn't a natural at walking on crutches. He actually moved faster when he was just dragging his leg. His arms were not used to carrying the bulk of his weight, and this was made evident as he labored through the hallways of the hospital. It took him fifteen minutes to get to the front door and another thirty to hobble to the Burger King down the street. He began to notice empathetic looks of concern from the people who saw him. He made his way to the bus stop. Some people saw the vulture flying around him. Some wondered, out loud, if there was a correlation between the broken man and the bird.

Jack saw the bus and increased his row-like crutching motion marginally. There was no way he was going to make it. His feeble desperation must have been unmistakable from thirty meters away, because the driver rumbled the big, red bus forward and stopped to pick him up—even without Jack making an overt gesture asking him to do so. He was astonished.

Bones followed the bus and the limping Jack back to his apartment. She waited outside, her strength fading. She would be dead from starvation, soon. She just wanted to be next to him. She would die next to him, so he could see what he had done.

The apartment was how he left it, Friday morning. Jack pressed play on the CD player. He undressed and wrapped his leg in a garbage bag and taped it up so he could take a bath. He kept seeing Layla's face in his drawings of Wings around the apartment, and he thought about his kite blowing away in the wind. After his shower, Jack unwrapped the cast, put on a fresh pair of boxers, and crawled into bed. He was clean, alive, and exhausted. He fell asleep without noticing Bones' silhouette in the curtains, as she perched on the balcony railing outside. It was 1:30 P.M..

CHAPTER 39
GETAWAY, 2:13 P.M.

When Bridget entered the bedroom, Jack was asleep. He was wearing blue boxers with white snowflakes, and his blue leg cast. His bed sheet was twirled around his body like a dissipating tornado. She went over and pulled back the curtain to let in the daylight. The apartment cast a long, rectangular shadow over the back courtyard.

"Holy crap, mate! It's a quarter past two and you're still in bed!" Bridget's voice pierced Jack's unconsciousness. He groaned into his pillow. "Oh, God! What happened to your leg?" Bridget questioned. Jack responded by repeating his moan a little louder. Bridget stood over him, wearing shorts and a faded, red t-shirt. He knew she was there. She placed her hands on the back of his shoulders and firmly pushed him twice into the mattress.

"What?" He whined, as his body bounced, slightly.

"What do you mean '*What*'? I just dragged my happy ass back from freaking Manchester because I promised I'd give you a haircut that you don't even really need. You should be kissing my ass, right now; not moaning at me. Wake up. What happened to your leg?"

Jack closed his eyes and thought about it. Then, he thought what it would be like to have sex with Bridget.

"What are you smiling about?" Bridget asked. "Come on, now, get up. I'll set my stuff up in the bathroom." Jack's leg hurt and he was tired, but he got up without complaining further. Bridget went into the bathroom while Jack got out of bed and hopped over.

Bridget cut Jack's hair, as he recounted the story. It was definitely the most engaging conversation the two had ever had. She asked him questions and they laughed together, especially about Layla. Bridget could sense how much Jack liked Layla—it made her unexpectedly jealous.

After fifteen minutes, Jack's hair was cut, and Bridget stood with her scissors at her side, listening as he finished his story. She brushed the hair off Jack's neck, and he stood up. He was a few centimeters taller than Bridget when she wasn't wearing heels. He reached around her and grabbed the broom against the wall to sweep the hair clippings off the bathroom floor.

"I think that's it. Then, I got into bed," he said, finishing his story.

"So, you were totally just falling asleep when I got home?! Wow." Bridget frowned, pretending to be sorry, "I'm sorry."

She studied him for a moment, turned and faced the door with her back towards him, crossed her arms, and pulled her shirt over her head and off her body. Jack stopped sweeping. Bridget used her arm to hold back her breasts, then looked at him over her shoulder.

"Oiy, that wasn't free! Your hands aren't broken. I want my back massage." Bridget walked into Jack's bedroom and laid face-down on his bed. This was a much more provocative choice in location than their usual haircut and massage exchanges—normally spent watching TV, on the couch. Jack felt the unusual sensation that Bridget was flirting with him, and he wasn't sure what to do. He finished sweeping.

"Where's your lotion?" he shouted, from the bathroom.

"It's in the bedroom, on the dresser."

Jack hopped on his good foot to Bridget's room, like a one-legged rabbit. "I don't see it."

"Maybe it's in the hall."

"You're killing me, Bridget."

"Sort it out, man!"

Hop, hop, hop, hop, hop, and hop.

"I just heard a gnarly-sounding accident, outside!" Bridget yelled from his bed.

"Got it!" Jack shouted back, *hop, hop, hop, hop, hop, and hop.*

Jack stood in the doorway, looking at the soft light on the dark, tan skin of Bridget's back, as she laid peacefully, stomach-down, with her head on Jack's pillow. *Hop, hop.* She felt him as he got onto the bed and straddled her back. His knees dug into the bed against her thighs. He sat back once, then lifted his weight off her. She felt his cast against her thigh.

Then, she felt the chill of the lotion and the unexpected strength in Jack's fingers. A second later: pleasure—he was getting *good*. Bridget moaned, softly. She *loved* getting back rubs. She started to think about work, moaned again, and stopped thinking about work. She thought about the American pushing his fingers into her lower back, moaned, and kept thinking about him instead of work.

Jack thought, as well, as he finger-painted on the muscles of her back. He knew what he was doing. He'd heard it in his own voice and knew where this particular situation was headed. It wasn't a wise choice. It wasn't even a good one— they were roommates that barely got along, and most of the time, they drove one another crazy. Bridget reached her hand behind her and grabbed the growing erection between Jack's legs. *Fuck it*, Jack concluded.

Passion is dormant in all of us, and once activated, it corrupts most rational decision-making processes. Jack leaned forward and kissed Bridget softly, on the back of her neck. A string of her hair stuck to his lip. He kissed Bridget's smooth, warm skin, again. She turned to lie on her back.

The lotion on her shoulder caressed past his neck. Her breasts pushed against his chest. She raised her pelvis and stomach to meet his and brought their weight to the middle of the bed.

Their eyes shut, and they kissed hard, then soft, then medium, then soft, and hard again. Their bodies mimicked the fluctuating pressure of their tongues and lips. They both had their eyes closed when Jack began to fantasize about Layla. He wrapped his fingers around the waist of Bridget's shorts and panties like they were a rip cord. She wrapped her arm around his neck to pull herself up to his ear before she opened her eyes.

EEEEeeeek! Bridget's shrill scream of terror landed directly into Jack's ear. He hurled himself from her, simultaneously cupping his ear, cursing, and finally losing his balance before falling off the single bed, dragging half the sheet with him to the floor. Outside, on the railing—with her cape of feathers towering over them—the vulture squawked, hissed, and beat her wings furiously in protest.

"Fuckin' hell, Jack!" Bridget was back to normal, "Your bird just scared the piss out of me. Sort this shit out, man. I've got to go to the bloody bathroom, now." The moment was completely lost. "Call someone, already! Jesus, Jack." He thought about what to do, then pulled himself off the ground and sat on the side of the bed. He stared at Bones on the other side of the glass. The large, dark bird had calmed down. She began to stare at the pictures in his room. The pictures of her and him in their dreams—she'd never seen them before.

Jack remembered the voice of Wings in his mind, "*I'm going to do all I can to get us together—but if you reject this person, or don't try, I'll be stuck with them, and without you.*"

Jack looked around the room, too. Every picture and painting were screaming her name to him. He stared at the vulture for another moment, then made his decision.

CHAPTER 40
FINALE, 5:00 P.M.

Once Jack made up his mind to be spontaneous, he based every decision he made on the objective of getting to the airport as quickly as possible. Unburdened by rational thought, adequate packing, and farewells, he made excellent time to Heathrow. Jack was confident that he had successfully deduced which flight Layla would be on by cross-referencing their conversations with the departing flight chart. He was standing in line and his thoughts finally slowed down. He began to think about what he was doing. He had an hour and twenty minutes until the departure, and one bag to check. He probably could have taken more consideration in packing, folding the clothes, and perhaps using the compartments more efficiently. He inched forward in the line, waiting to talk to a ticket agent. Even though he had packed as lightly as he could to accommodate his broken right leg, his bag was still heavy. For a moment, he realized his plan might not work. He didn't even try to hook-up with Bridget again. He could have probably been back at their apartment having sex with her, at this very moment.

It was Jack's turn in line. The ticket agent was in her forties, with an eighties-style perm. She welcomed Jack with the face of a mother. He politely lied, explaining that his fiancé would be on the flight, and he requested a seat next to her so that he could surprise her. The woman explained that she couldn't give out passenger information, and then winked like she did something illegal.

This promptly reminded Jack that Layla had said she included a first-class ticket home as the best way to end a vacation. The seat next to her ended up costing him an uncomfortable chunk of his vacation fund. Jack smiled to himself in anticipation—he'd never flown first-class, before. He hobbled his way to the McDonald's, after passing through security. The breakfast menu was still available, and Jack certainly didn't complain. He debated whether to eat his sausage McGriddle right away, but he was nervous and didn't want his breath to smell like pig meat, cornflower, and syrup. He wished for a breath mint, but none appeared, so he held off on eating the sandwich. He rowed and hopped with his crutches down the terminal to the gate, holding the bag of McDonald's.

He saw Layla from behind. She was wearing a backpack and had a small, rolling suitcase by her side. Her eyes were cast out over the runway. Jack's heart raced. He hobbled up behind her, then made sure to speak clearly, so he wouldn't have to repeat himself, "So I've been thinking…"

Layla turned to face him, and Jack noticed what she had been transfixed on. Bones the vulture, circling above the plane, outside. "You've got to be shitting me," Jack said. Layla, who had the same thought a few minutes before, was staring at Jack, wondering why he was there. By the look of bewilderment on his face studying the bird, it seemed as if, for the moment, he was wondering why he was there, too.

"Jack! What are you doing here? What happened to your leg?" Layla interrogated him, while he blinked himself back to the moment. "Are you sta…, sta…, looking for me? Seriously, dude, are you stalking me?

"Good questions," Jack was flustered.

"Yeah, they are. What happened to your leg?" She

repeated.

"I accidently broke it, last night," he said. They looked at his leg. "I broke my front tooth out, too." Jack declared, while they were on the subject, but then regretted mentioning it as it further displaced him from the reason he was there.

"You broke your tooth, too?"

"Yeah, this one," Jack pointed at his right, front tooth. Layla inspected.

"Looks good," she stepped back. "Did you get a haircut, too?" He smirked and nodded yes. "You've been busy, haven't you? What sort of accident?"

"I got punched."

"In the tooth?"

"No," Jack said.

"In your leg?"

"No, I'll tell you all about it. How about we go back to your original question."

"Okay, that's a good idea. So, what brings you and the vulture to the airport?"

Jack smiled, "I have a crush on you. That's why I'm here. I told you that your haircut was from a dream, but I don't care about that shit. I know it's a crazy way to meet someone in the first place, but I can't untangle the knot of real feelings I have for you from this experience. I can't un-laugh or un-live every little moment that has compelled me to be here. I mean…how could just a couple of days mean so much to me? I don't want to apologize for being here. This is just where I want to be. Hanging out with you, even if it's just for a couple more hours." Layla was flattered and smiled. Jack mistook this as a cue that he should keep talking, "See, I don't need to have long, passionate, sweaty sex with you to validate the experience of knowing you as a person, either." Jack heard himself and immediately knew that this last, awkward statement had missed the mark.

"Did you track me to this flight to tell me that you *don't* want to have sex with me?" Layla asked, jumping on his misstep.

"I don't think so." Jack backtracked, "I wasn't taking the sweaty sex off the table. It's just that I was…"

"May I?" Layla said, and Jack listened closely. "I'm going to do us a favor and not overreact. Honestly, I don't know what to think, yet. What would you think? Its sweet, Jack, profoundly sweet. I can say that. Your bird is here," said Layla.

"I noticed."

"She showed up a couple minutes ago." Layla looked back at Jack, "I will say this, for now: up until the end, that was the most romantic speech I've ever heard from a man on crutches, waving around a bag of McDonald's. It kind of grossed me out a little bit."

Jack grimaced and sat down. His crutches were propped between his legs, like aluminum stalks of corn. Layla sat next to him. He opened his breakfast, and they watched Bones for a moment.

As they sat there waiting to board the plane, Jack explained how he and Dustin ended up in a fight, and how his tooth was broken before his leg. Jack confessed that he had canceled his trip to Greece in the hopes that he could spend the vacation in New York, living off disability, while trying to get Layla to fall in love with him before he ran out of money. Layla told Jack about her trip up to Oxford. A tangential conversation about winter sports featured Layla's claim that she was Van Damme on a snowboard.

As they boarded the plane, scuttled to their seats, and stowed their luggage, Jack told Layla of his desire to own a catfish—obviously, in a large tank. He said this specifically, so he could tell everyone that he owned a cat.

The plush, blue leather, first-class chairs felt like thrones as they took their seats. Everything was going great.

"Listen, Chestnut! We are not getting a catfish."

"Fine. Morris is out. How about a sea horse? I can tell people I own a horse."

"Maybe. You know seahorses are tiny, right?"

"I have seen *The Snorks*," Jack paused. "That was the first time you have referred to us as 'we.'"

Layla realized this pronoun slip, but felt baited, and didn't respond. She turned her attention to the passengers around them who were giving commentary and observations regarding the vulture outside the plane.

Jack and Layla failed to notice the commotion at the front of the aircraft. It was Dustin Switch. He was strung-out, wearing the same clothes as the night before, except for a different, inside-out T-shirt; oversized sunglasses; and five, shimmering, plastic beaded necklaces dangling from his neck. He saw Jack, straightaway.

"Holy shit. We got a party now! Jack!" Dustin yelled. Jack wanted to slap himself on the forehead but didn't. "I did break your leg! What the hell are you doing on my plane? In first-class?! You're the poorest guy that I hang out with. Who are you trying to impress?" Dustin noticed Layla. "Hey. I know you. Wow! The paparazzi from the elevator. Bridget really fucked up your hair." Jack and Layla both frowned. Dustin looked at them, together. "This is the chick you were talking about? Layla! No way! You did chase after her! How's it going?"

Jack found himself unable to answer the cross-examination. It was too abrupt, and it spoiled everything. He looked back at Layla—she calmed him. Dustin watched them and was about to say something awful, but before he could, Bones flew past the windows of the plane like an angry, feathered stunt jet. Dustin and Jack quickly recoiled. Layla turned as a couple of people screamed, and she caught the end of the swoop.

"I told you, Jack! That bird is after me. It's relentless," Dustin shouted. Jack leaned over to talk to him.

"She is harmless. Stop being an ass. Once we take off, she'll be gone. Now sit down! There are people behind you. I'll talk to you in a couple minutes."

The captain came over the intercom, "*Good evening, folks. This is Captain McMasters speaking. Sorry about the little delay, here. It appears a rather large bird has taken a liking to our airplane,"* the captain gave a nervous chuckle. *"We are going to have our ground crew scare her off real quick, then we'll be on our way."*

The passengers watched carefully. Two crewmen with florescent orange earphones on, riding in a small, yellow buggy, approached Flight 386. The crewman riding shotgun held an air-horn like it was a canister of hornet spray, and defensively pointed it at the vulture. The sharp blast—while muffled by the sounds of the airplane—was still audible inside the 747. The startled bird quickly flew high over the terminal. The buggy left, the captain started the engines, and Jack felt an absolute freedom from the mysterious and creepy bird.

The plane moved forward and around the curve of the taxiway. Across the aisle from Jack and Layla, Dustin rested his head against the back of the seat.

"I get really nervous at take-off," Layla softly said to Jack, looking out the window.

"I do, too," he replied. "We can hold hands if you want."

"Oh, my God! You guys are so gay!" Dustin shouted at the ceiling of the plane. He turned his head to face them from across the aisle. Jack and Layla glared at him, "Never mind," he said, then went back to looking at the ceiling with his eyes closed behind his large, dark glasses. The plane was now in position for take-off. Layla looked at Jack.

"Jack, this is all happening too fast. I can see what you want, and it's not to just be buddies. What if I feel pushed? I don't want you, or anyone, to rush me into a relationship. I take these things seriously. First, there is a world of stuff that you don't even know about me, and just as many that I don't know about you. Jack, my name isn't even Layla, its Michaela. That isn't that important. It's just an example of something pretty significant all my friends know. It's actually pretty insulting that you think I'm so transparent, that based on one night of flirting, you could be so confident of our long-term compatibility. I can be a real bitch, and it is not funny. How are you going to handle that?" she paused, "I have herpes, too." Jack's jaw dropped and his stomach sank. Dustin, who was enjoying her commentary, stopped and looked over in disbelief. "I'm kidding, you assholes, but that's my point!" Jack was discouraged by her speech, but not angry. She had made some important arguments. He was no stranger to defeat. He smiled softly and said,

"Okay," then he put his hand on the armrest, palm up, fingers open. The force of the plane kicked them back a little, into their seats, and Layla's fingers locked into his.

Flight 386 lifted off the ground. It was in flight only a few seconds before the vulture ripped past the plane that was flying at two hundred miles per hour, through the left engine.

The explosion prompted an orchestra of screaming, praying, and general terror. Oxygen masks were suddenly dangling in the cabin like little tether balls.

A moment later, they would be dead. Jack's natural, pessimistic disposition allowed him to stay calm and soak it all in without drawing any additional attention to himself.

The plane veered left, creating a centrifuge of force inside the aircraft. Layla's lips quivered and the force of the plane's looping descent pulled a couple of tears towards her ears.

Jack watched her, then shouted what would be his last words,

"This could be worse," he paused. "We could be in coach!" Layla snickered, which is very rare on a plane full of people about to die. Jack swallowed. Layla held his hand tight. He held hers and they prepared to hit the ground.

"Tell the world my story!" Dustin's godless last words roared triumphantly over the screams and prayers.

Meanwhile—in the cockpit—Captain Michael "Black Baron" McMasters Jr. had his own conclusion in mind and had not resigned to a witty demise. A split second after the explosion, he had already cut the right engine and begun to compensate the left throttle and rudders. Under tremendous g-forces, he reinitiated the landing gear. He was quickly losing altitude. He surveyed the ground below for a place to crash-land. He knew the impact trajectory for the situation and felt the curving median of the M4 highway he was looking at, which ran past the airport, might have just enough room to land the plane. *I'll make it enough space.* He didn't plan on missing his daughter, Mariana's, 5th birthday—or the median. The yoke in his left hand began to bend.

Traffic was congested, for a Sunday. The impact sounded like a freight train had dropped from the sky, and the explosion sent a massive fireball down the center of the M4, drowning out the life in its path with burning fuel and shrapnel. Everyone onboard, seventy motorists, and the vulture died in seconds. Special reports and stories of the victims flooded the news—including profiles of McMasters, Dustin, and even a respected neurosurgeon that was in coach. While the truth of what happened at this point is obvious, at the time, it was not necessarily accessible or believable information. Currently, there is no accounting for the supernatural in modern, credible journalism.

The chaos after the plane crash left the militant terrorist groups scratching their heads and pointing fingers at one another, while the Federal Aviation Administration seized the opportunity to arbitrarily ban containers of liquid greater than 3.4 ounces from all flights. In the end, the world was less affected by the actual and earnest tragedy of the crash, and more directly affected by its polarization of international tensions and the regulations born from it. *C'est la vie, qu'est ce qu'on peut y faire.*

EPILOGUE
REQUIEM

Jack stared down at the water below him, from the Olympic platform diving board. There was no way down. He was six years old, he was scared, and he thought he was alone. When he turned around looking for a way out, he found there was also a little girl there, in a blue dress. She had a confused look on her face.

"Who are you?" he asked, as she stepped forward to survey the quagmire.

"I don't remember." she said.

"Well, my name is Jack, and this is my dream. How did you get here?"

"Nice to meet you, Jack. I don't know. I don't know how I got here. I just woke up here."

"Maybe you're an angel."

"I don't think so. Don't they have beautiful wings?"

"Well, put your arms up, like you're a bird."

"Like this?" She extended her arms out, flapped them a few times, and then began to laugh at herself.

"See, there you go: wings," he said. "Now, you can be an angel, if you want."

"You're funny," she said, "But I still can't fly. How are we going to get off this diving board? I'm scared." Jack thought for a second, then said,

159

"I'm afraid, too. We should jump together—in case something bad happens."

THE END

The Big Adventures of a Salty Little Man

PART I: 1999
CHAPTER 1

Well, to start, I made it to Europe alive. I arrived in Paris at six-thirty in the morning. It was, and remains, much colder than I anticipated. I've resorted to using the blanket I took from the airplane as a scarf, and I look absurd.

I had fourteen hours to kill before my train was scheduled to leave for Salzburg. I walked across Paris randomly filming things. Unfortunately, that didn't take fourteen hours and I was exhausted. I used my remaining time in Paris to sleep on the floor of the train station, temporarily preventing vagrants from urinating on the area where I was lying...I hope. My overnight train connects in Munich (München), so there is a one-hundred percent chance I will disembark for some German adult beverages. I haven't spoken in two days, which is an odd, but interesting feeling.

CHAPTER 2

Munich was overcast but warm while I was there. I visited the BMW Museum/Corporate Head Quarters. The reception area was loaded with superfluous lights and buttons, which made it look like the engine room from a 1970's Star Trek Episode. I don't know shit about cars, so the whole tour was essentially as rewarding to me as paying fifteen dollars to climb a seven-story winding ramp.

After the tour, I revisited the nearby site of the 1972 Olympics. I took in the natural beauty while making a strenuous climb up a steep hill but hurt my knee like a feeble, old person and have been hobbling around ever since.

On one hand, the Germans seem very jolly, but at the same time, I've observed the language is extremely guttural and the tone can be hard to discern. Listening to a conversation reminds me of someone trying to tell a story with food in their mouth, but they are also becoming exceedingly frustrated because nobody can understand them.

I went to the local tourist office to inquire about nearby beer gardens. After asking, the man behind the desk immediately looked at me like I was insane and pointed outside, saying, "Are you crazy? People don't go to the beer gardens when the weather is like this!"

Sure, it was a tiny bit overcast…but come on! He evidently did not realize the man with whom he was dealing. I once drove through a hurricane for free PBR and a two percent chance of meeting a girl. I studied the sky; no tornados of blood, no werewolves running around the streets dismembering people. I was ready to party.

A round of German beers weighs approximately fifty-five pounds. I'm not convinced this is a sensible serving size. However, while I was deadlifting the giant beer stein to my face, I decided to analyze it further by projecting a conversation between the barmen and a regular customer.

Otto approaches the bar and says, "Gunter! You cow. Are you pregnant, or just fat as usual? Don't answer that; just get me a draft beer, buddy."

Gunter, sensitive about his weight, just stares at Otto for a moment. Then, he says, "Would you like one or two gallons of beer."

"Better make that just the one gallon. I have a long drive."

Gunter grabs a glass. The beer starts flowing out of the bathtub-grade faucet, and he desperately wants to tell Otto that he thinks his shorts are stupid-looking and outdated.

On the morning of my departure, I decided to get the "all you can eat" breakfast from the hostel where I stayed. The only things I recognized were the bread, jelly, sauerkraut, and the napkins. Beyond the kraut, there were about six other things that I would have rather poked with a stick than put in my mouth. They looked as appetizing as pinecone meat or a handful of used rubber gloves. Regardless, I found the "all you can eat" to be less of an invitation and more of a challenge. On to Austria I go.re.

CHAPTER 3

Salzburg, the home of Mozart, Hitler, and salt. It was overcast like Germany, but much colder, which gave it an eerie feeling. What was also eerie for the residents was me hobbling through the streets, lost, and looking for my hostel. The place was marvelous when I found it. They offered twenty-five schilling beers, which converts to approximately one pair of Goodwill socks per beer.

I took a bus tour, and it did not go well. I couldn't understand anything the driver was trying to say. I eventually gave up, stared out the window, and waited for it to end. On my mother's recommendation, I toured the salt mine, and it was worth it. On my personal recommendation, I went to the St. Augustine Beer Garden and Brewery, located conveniently across the street from the hospital. I had thought I'd seen it all in Germany, but this place took it to the next level. This house of worship offered five-liter beers. The mug, itself, was gargantuan, like a ceramic oil drum. I stared at it for at least a minute. My wallet, liver, and my arms agreed that we couldn't afford it. I wasn't sure I'd be able to lift it and carry it to the table without severely injuring myself. I went with the modest one-liter.

Meanwhile, the floor was thoroughly soaked with beer

because the salty Austrian behind the counter wouldn't stop pouring it until the beer was overflowing out of the mug for at least five seconds. He immediately chucked me the sloppy mess, and before I even knew what was going on, he had the nerve to yell, "Drink za beer! Don't wash ze floor with it! Ha ha ha."

I wasn't amused.

CHAPTER 4

I've moved into my apartment and started school in Italy, and it is pretty cool. I think the stairs were imported from Egypt; not because they are old, but because they are massive blocks that look like they came from the pyramids. I have to climb them by heaving one leg over the lip, then hoisting my body over onto each step. Unfortunately, there are about forty-five of the damned things between the ground floor and my apartment.

There is a seven-to-one girl-to-guy ratio at my school. This means I will fall in love with at least four of the girls and still be a virgin in three months. Furthermore, I had a bag of valuables stolen from me while I was sleeping at the train station like a hobo because I wanted to go out and spend my money partying instead of getting a proper hotel room.

As I started school, Dustin showed up from left field with friends, and suddenly the first week of school was less about education and all about trying to meet girls and plan a road trip (as first weeks of college often are). We were extremely successful at meeting girls…

To combat sophisticated bi-lingual European women having conversations about us that we couldn't understand,

Dustin and I would turn the tables and talk to each other using rap and hip-hop terminology. Before we knew it, it was time to head to the Swiss Alps.

For me, the train ride to Switzerland was peaceful. Thanks to a healthy dose of whiskey, I missed a late-night door-to-door manhunt at the border. I also missed my "friends" conspiring to choke me to death for snoring the whole evening. Thanks to the whiskey, when I awoke, the only evidence of the manhunt was that my backpack full of toenail clippings and Barbie dolls had gotten dumped out during the search, and nobody would look at me. Regardless, I got to Switzerland feeling spunky.

We arrived at our destination around eight. Balmer's (our hostel) had a complimentary shuttle to pick people up at the train station, which scored high marks in my book. The hostel was only about a mile down the road. Yet, in that short distance, our weird shuttle driver managed to go from zero-to-slimeball in three seconds by repeatedly offering lodgings at his place to any girls in the van that didn't want to pay twenty dollars for the hostel. It was a *little* unprofessional in my opinion.

Some people went on adventures: horseback riding, skydiving, and bungee jumping. Trip and I bought a bunch of weed from the store and played free foosball until we were sweating. Later, we ran into a group of kids from FSU. I tried to talk to them, but they brushed me off like I was a stinky vagrant trying to throw my hobo sleeping bag over their shoulders like a cape. Of course, I was so stoned that I was probably attempting to introduce myself to a seesaw and a row of hedges.

Our next move as a group was sixteen-hundred feet above sea level to the scenic village of Murren. Nestled into the side of the mountain, it offers a breathtaking above-the-clouds view of the Alps. Meanwhile, we bought too much fancy pot for five people to casually smoke. Dustin and I had seen this sort of thing before, in Amsterdam. I'll spare you the antics to protect the guilty. However, we didn't throw it out; we didn't take any of it with us; and we ate a lot of onion rings. School is starting to get real so I will be in touch when the dust clears.

CHAPTER 5

School is going well. I've made some good friends. They invited me to join them on their trip to the French Riviera. As the plan started to develop, I realized that we had different priorities. While they were looking up luxury hotels, I was looking up places where I could donate plasma and semen for cash. Instead of joining in on their plans, I decided to join them indirectly, with a more economical vacation loosely based on what I would do if I had money.

Phase One of the plan was taking the overnight train from Florence, Italy to Monaco, to forego the cost of a hotel room. *Phase Two* was me strategically drinking enough to have a good time on my train, leaving at midnight. *Phase Three* was a shit-show because I drank way too many gin & tonics during *Phase Two* and left my apartment seeing double. Furthermore, while I was in high spirits, I remembered a Visa commercial from when I was younger and decided that since my pants converted into shorts, I was wearing two outfits and didn't need any other clothes weighing me down. So, I left the apartment with relevant documents, a CD player, one CD, a camera, a journal, and toiletries. After rumbling, stumbling, and fumbling my way to the train station, I staggered to my seat and passed out.

173

Phase Four was not planned for at all. This was when I was unexpectedly woken up, still very drunk, about two hours later. I was utterly confused. The first thing I could gather from the angry people yelling at me was that I was supposed to wake up so I could get off the train. I switched to a much smaller, already full car, where I had to ride out my drunkenness sitting in a hallway with people trying to get by in both directions. It was unpleasant. I was also now sweating alcohol like Elvis and completely dehydrated. Did I mention that my new home was sweltering and basically smelled like a dead man's nut-sack? The freshest air I had in four hours was when some old guido crop-dusted me on his way to the bathroom.

Finally, I arrived in Monte Carlo. As usual, when I went to the information desk, the lady working eyeballed me like I was a lunatic. I asked why it was so hard to find a room in town, and she just rolled her eyes. I went outside, and it sounded like the city was being attacked by giant hornets. It turns out that it was the weekend of the Monaco Grand Prix. It was incredible watching the cars zip through the tiny European streets. There were even some places that it was free to look at the race; namely, "Spectator Decapitation Turn" sponsored by *Faces of Death*, located near the bakery. I decided it was time to move on when Dr. B. Gross asked me to sign a video consent and release form.

In Monaco, the conversion rate is six-and-a-half Franks to one US Dollar, which makes everything seem even more expensive than it is. This, coincidentally, is also the only place where I've ordered a ham sandwich and was given a sandwich that was composed of just bread and ham. I left lunch disappointed with the lingering feeling that I'd been hornswoggled.

Next, I decided to test my luck at the world-famous Casino Monte Carlo, featured in several Bond movies and the 1991 classic, *If Looks Could Kill*, starring the late Richard Grieco. It was my first time in a casino, so I was pretty nervous. I took out three hundred Franks, then immediately went to the roulette table, trembling and covered in sweat. I bet all my Franks on black and won! It was a glorious eight minutes before I lost it all back to the house. So, I decided to get to the train station and head for Nice.

I did not have a good time in Nice. I was looking for one particular place and couldn't find it; and after a couple hours, when I tried to get back to the train station, I couldn't find that, either. It was miserable. There were two good things about Nice, because despite concerns about rampant mad cow disease, there is no meat from a steer which I fear. Last time I checked, Dustin and I are still in an active European Hamburger Eating Contest, and if I slack for a day, he might wolf down three just to pad the lead a little. Did I say two good things about Nice? I meant one.

Speaking of Dustin; Trip, Jon, and he were in Spain, heading for Paris. My friends, Lauren and Laura, were already in Paris, and the last/only train leaving Nice was to Paris. I got there Saturday morning, checked into my hostel, and decided I wanted to go see Normandy; but seven hours and five train stations later, I realized I wasn't going to make it and turned back.

The hostel I stayed at was agreeable, but the neighborhood made me nervous. The road was unpaved, which seemed strange for being in central Paris. I thought that maybe it was to help cut down on the drive-by shootings but then realized that French cars are made of aluminum foil and wood glue, and if you fired a gun out of the window, the kick-back would be liable to flip the vehicle..

CHAPTER 6

It's been a little over a month since I've written, so there's some catching-up to do. I'd like to start with Venice. Venice was great. There is a lot of water there, but not as much as the tears I cry when I take off my shirt. I prefer streets because you can cross them without a bridge. Furthermore, even though the canals are narrow, the bridges are steep and pronounced arcs. The only reason I can gather for this extra legwork is so the beret-wearing, mime-ish looking swindlers in the canoes (AKA the Gondoliers), wouldn't have to bend over too much while rowing tourists around in circles like inexperienced taxi drivers.

In my extensively limited experience with European travel, I nominate Venice as having the poorest nightlife, thus far. It was easier to find a beer during prohibition. If you were fortunate enough to grease a few palms and get the name of a place that was open later than 9:30 P.M., you would certainly be dismayed when the interior was a hundred degrees Celsius, and the bartender had both gray hair and a hairnet. I didn't know if she was going to bring me a sloppy joe and some tater tots or a Heineken.

Moving on…Rome. I've never seen a place so outdated. There's nothing more pathetic than two tourist attractions competing for which is older. Over to your left, it looks like the last Motel 6 on the border of Iraq and Syria. On the right side of you, there is a fence surrounding a ginormous ant hill and some crabgrass, with a man outside the wall trying to sell you a picture of what things used to look like in that location three-thousand years ago. It is the most depressing Central Business District I have ever seen.

While I was in Rome, we visited the Vatican. Holy shit. I mean, I'm Catholic as fuck, and I was really thrilled to see the "Big House." However, in the spirit of things, I had a few issues. I thought it was supposed to be a religious center. There was so much treasure and stolen artifacts that the place looked less like a house of spiritual worship and more like One-Eyed Willy's Pirate Ship from *The Goonies*. Meanwhile, it was hotter than a German bathhouse in there and all I could think while staring at a four-thousand-year-old statue lifted from the Greeks, sweat dripping down my brow, was that somebody needs to get JC some A/C. Seriously, you'd think with all of their priceless stolen decorations, someone in the Holy See could squeak out a deal for some HVAC units.

Florence was my home base for the summer. University felt much like school the whole time but all-in-all, it was a necessary evil; one which, I like to think, if pursued, might help me find an excellent job someday. The current alternative is to drink myself to death on a couch made of filled trash bags.

I had booked my return flight for two months after school had ended. My plan was to travel to Ireland and do some side-work for an old family friend. Meanwhile, a group of fellow students that I had become friends with expected to return to Switzerland as an end-of-semester adventure, and I tagged along. When I saw the "Help Wanted" sign at the Balmer's youth hostel, I applied, and they gave me the job. Bam! I start tomorrow. To be continued.

CHAPTER 7

I've been working at Balmer's for a little over a month. I mostly make beds and mop floors. It kind of feels like I live in an orphanage for alcoholics and extreme sports fans that don't want to grow up. Furthermore, working illegally as a migrant worker in a foreign country is an exciting experience, especially in Switzerland. To avoid suspicion, I've begun wearing a green suede vest, Robin Hood-style cap, and started yodeling the national anthem if someone tries to speak to me in anything but English (which is ninety percent of the time I'm not at work).

You may be interested in how the Swiss dominate recycling; how they have a seemingly perfect balance of preserving the rich, natural beauty while providing a world-class infrastructure; that they have been living in peace with three different national languages for seven hundred years. However, that shit isn't funny.

So, there are like a hundred Koreans staying at the youth hostel. I find these Koreans stereotypically tiny and enthusiastic, like cocker spaniels. I had to dig a little deeper into this inexplicable jubilation over things like free water, the sky, and bowls of cornflakes. My first hypothesis: South Korea must be an incredibly boring place. Then, I realized they are just happy to be alive and as far away from North Korea as they can get. The U.S. has it easy. The Canadians? Mexicans? Laughable threats. South Korea, however, is on a peninsula of terror surrounded by China, Japan, North Korea and the Pacific Ocean. How they exist is in itself a mystery. Perhaps smiling and frantically waving peace signs at everyone has helped them circumvent natural selection.

We just had "Swiss Day," which is Switzerland's largest holiday. To celebrate, Balmer's staff took shots of liquor before work. What could go wrong with such a great idea? An ill omen was seeing the bottle of Jägermeister ravaged like a pepperoni pizza being thrown to a pack of feral dogs. I held my own, but not as much can be said for everyone else. Benny lost his job; he was too drunk to make beds. Annette jumped off a bridge and broke a bone in her back.

Honestly, despite working at Balmer's for the past two months, I must say my new job skill column has been limited. I now can roll excellent joints, I can also open beer bottles with a lighter, and brew iced coffee by the pot. These are the trades I will be bragging about to the people around me while I'm waiting in line for vegetable soup and an opportunity to rummage a clothes pile for a free pair of used sweatpants.

Finally, I spent the last two weeks with the most amazing Polish-Argentinian, named Rosa. My prayers are that Rosa will be coming to the States in the next couple of months so our child can be born an American citizen. Just kidding. I'm still a virgin.

PART II: 2000
CHAPTER 8

I'm rapidly approaching my sixth month in Europe and thought I'd give everyone an update. I lost my virginity. My plan was to get a prostitute when we got to Amsterdam. However, I gave it away the previous day to a young, Irish woman. Sex is surprisingly more labor-intensive than I imagined...I also wasn't very good at it (in case that wasn't evident from the first clause of that sentence). I felt like a one-man band who had no idea how to actually play his instruments. I definitely produced more excuses than orgasms.

Interlaken was eventful. Nobody got the jobs they were expecting. Dustin eventually became a nanny. I got fired on my day off while wearing a dress, but successfully pleaded my way back into good graces. Chris and Curtis survived basically by recycling, foraging, and crafting walking sticks from branches. I've already dedicated myself to writing a full account addressing the mischiefs that have transpired on this trip. In other words, I'll get back to that later.

Meanwhile, Dustin and I are settling into our apartment in Italy with ease. You may wonder, since it is my third semester in Italy, do I speak Italian? Let me address this.

The fundamental importance of language is for people to communicate with one another. I live in the heart of Florence, Italy. However, my day-to-day life is not spent haggling in Italian with a local street vendor over the price of an avocado that I think is too expensive. I'm not a chit-chatter. I don't sit at a café talking and laughing with my local Italian buddies about the big football game coming up. In fact, most of my interactions are with the Italian mosquito population, which comes from all parts of the *Centro Classico* to feast on my American blood and procreate in the unreachable crevices of our apartment's ten-foot ceilings.

I'm not saying that the Italian language is bad or that there is something wrong with Italy. I'm merely making a statement in practicality: Italian is a dying language. It takes months to learn basic Italian; not accounting for regional dialects. In the heart of Italy, you can just as easily live in Florence day-to-day not knowing more than ten words in Italian as someone who doesn't speak any other language besides Italian. I'm saying, the time and effort in learning the native language of Italy doesn't add up to the benefit.

I go from place to place with every intention of putting my moderate Italian speech into practice (out of respect and an earnest desire to speak it), but before I even open my mouth, my Italian counterpart has already asked me something in English. Sixty million people in the world speak Italian, a giant 2% of the world's population. It's a dying language not because Italy is growing smaller, but because the world is growing bigger around it, and that world doesn't speak Italian.

Being an American taking an Italian language class was not a school-provided option until reaching college. I returned from Italy in 1997 with a solid B in Italian I under my belt, but then, there was only one section of Italian II for the entire university. Out of thirty thousand students, they could not fill two classrooms with enough people who wanted to learn Italian. I was crestfallen, plus I had far too little time and money to hold onto the idea that if I learned Italian, I'd actually use it.

Furthermore, with romance languages, we often find the problem of dialects. This means two people speaking Italian won't be able to understand each other. For someone who speaks Italian as a second language, this dialectic change could make years of school null simply because the speaker is from a different region of a country the same size as Florida. The listener could be as helpless to understand a conversation as someone who has little or no experience with Italian grammar.

I go through my day speaking fewer than ten words in Italian, simply because I don't have to. On a day where I wake up at 9:00, I walk to the café nearest my school and order "*un café e questa il pasta*," then, "*grazie*," then I go to school, then home for a nap, and back to school again until 5:15. I leave campus and walk across the street to use the internet. The only time I interact with someone there is when I leave, and the guy tells me how much I owe. That conversation involves me walking up to the counter and the mid-twenties Italian man with short, spiky hair saying, "Three euros," (in English, of course).

My last epic Italian encounter of most days happens at the Standa, a block from my house. I frugally pick out a couple things to eat, normally the ingredients for French toast. After standing in line for twenty minutes, the cashier rings me up and says "Bag?" not, "*una buosta*?" as he has said to everyone in front of me. Dejected, I say, "Yes," then take my groceries and go home.

I don't blame these people for speaking to me in English. God knows, I'm not an Italian man. I don't have a jean jacket and tight shirt. The Italians speak English to me because it makes their life easier, and that's great because that makes my life easier…so who's complaining? "This is their country. We should speak their language." I think there should be one language that everyone speaks. I don't care what language it is. If everyone wants to speak Swahili, then I'll gladly speak Swahili. The point is, I could go out of my way to speak Italian if I wanted to, but I'm in fucking Italy. I think I've gone far enough out of my way.

CHAPTER 9

Italy is cold and old, and I'm penniless. All I eat are egg sandwiches and French toast, which are basically the same fucking thing. In fact, I have cooked so much French toast this fall that I claim to be its undisputed champion (which, if you are keeping track, I also currently pretend to be the undisputed champion of running like a T-rex).

School is a bitch. I think the workload is a bit much. I feel like I'm at an actual college, instead of Florida State. Meanwhile, we just read *The Republic* in my Political Theory class. If you love repeatedly reading long sentences until they make sense, this is the book for you. Sure, in the end, it provided unbelievably vivid philosophical images. My problem is that everyone pretends to understand what Socrates was saying. Then, they just agree with him so the teacher can go on without asking for any clarification.

"Then is not that which is fulfilled of what more truly is, and which itself more truly is, more truly filled and satisfied than that which being itself less real is filled with more unreal things?" asked Socrates.

"No!" Jack Chestnut said, "Because, the concrete belief in something unreal could bring true happiness, while the real may only lead to a spiral of questions and emptiness that is the want for what you can't understand. Nah, man, I'm just fucking with you. I don't even really know what the fuck you are babbling about." Jack exhales a cloud of white smoke. "Man, Socks, this is some real shit! You said you got this from Sparta?"

I just got back from Rome about a week ago. It was fun. I got to know some of the people I go to school with a little better. This time, a highlight was our trip to the catacombs, a maze of underground tombs carved out by the early Christians. It is also the site of the 1976 Hide-and-Go-Seek Death Match Tournament; where legendary Doctor Invisible was finally killed by Ghost-face Erik, the albino Norwegian with no tongue.

In other news, *Jammy Jamm 2000: Sup Wit Dat Jam* is beginning to take form, although formal invitations haven't been sent out. Dustin and I plan on bringing a little tradition from home across to Italia. My newer friends should either be entertained or horrified by the party we throw. Of course, that depends on their open-mindedness towards horse-powered anal impalement…

I have provided my phone number, which is 333-942-5915. I'm giving this number out because I want to be the first person notified if Conrad is killed in a gruesome car accident. Any personal phone calls? Well, please not too late because that is when I'm masturbating to the stockpile of porn I downloaded while living in the States. You all called me a pervert, but who's laughing now?

While traveling, I have been exposed to increasing anti-American sentiment, regarding the growing strife in Iraq and the looming presence of Osama-Bomb-Alota. As far as I'm concerned, I grew up watching *G.I. Joe*, so COBRA makes Al-Qaeda look like *The Teletubbies*. COBRA didn't hijack a couple of planes; they took over full control of the world more than twice. I'm glad COBRA Commander wasn't screaming about a convoluted jihad. He was plainly saying, "Hey man, I have a snake head for a face, I'm a sadist, and look at all the evil people I hang out with! I want to take over the world; that's my thing. I'm insane." I was mentally predisposed to violence as a child by watching a gorgon trying to subjugate the world for no reason. Al-Qaeda? They're amateurs.

After school, I plan on spending the second half of December and all of January in Switzerland being a ski bum, then coming home for a couple of months before my London Invasion.

PART III: 2001
CHAPTER 10

London and I go together like a cat lady's house and the pungent smell of urine. I affectionately refer to my apartment as "The Pirate Ship." It is a "room-share" which means there are four beds in one room and three in the other (a girl's side and a guy's side). The floors all creak, there is a line to use everything, and the pointed front balcony and square rear balcony give a ship-like feel.

The crew includes:

• Me (laid back, charming, a blue ribbon smile with understated good looks and no mentionable sex life.)

• Kelly, a Tasmanian, (she has a very colorful character but is more aggravating than anything, similar to her taste in music, which officially is any song with an air raid siren and an electronic voice repeating words like "groove" or "energy").

• Alex, a hell of a nice guy from France (loves walking around in his boxers to show how much he works out...I don't blame him. I walk around in a hospital gown and nubby socks to show how anemic I am). The other day, Alex printed out some rap lyrics, and I had to translate them because "black people talk crazy," and rap songs are unintelligible even on paper. I'm sad to say that after four years of traveling, my translating skills are limited to explaining what "crunked-up" means to another man.

• Crystal and Girl-X: very cute French girls, but I don't see them much. Girl-X has been living in the apartment for ten days, and I don't even know her name.

• Brandon: he's an Aussie; a beanstalk schoolteacher. I would just prefer hearing less of his chipmunk voice complaining about everything. He and our seventh roommate don't get along so well.

• Dustin: I don't exactly know how I ended up living with this man, again. I'm happy for him; he just got a job at a bar called The Lamb. It's a funny name considering some of the unspeakable comments he has made about livestock since we have been friends.

Finding a well-paying job with a six-month work visa has reluctantly become a fairy tale for me. Most companies want a two-year visa. That's a pretty big commitment considering it only takes a couple of months before an employer realizes they hate me. At the moment, I work down the street from Buckingham Palace at a pub called The Cask and Glass. It is uniquely small; like serving beer in a double-wide port-a-john with carpeted floors and wood trim.

I can only afford to go out once a week, which is okay because Saturday night and Sunday are my only real times off work. I give one good effort at picking up a girl each Saturday, which generally fails. The drawback of liquid courage is that by the time I'm confident enough to talk to a girl, my eyes are bloodshot and hazy, I'm slurring, sweating, and I only have five dollars left to my name. Meanwhile, on the other night off, I like to go to the seediest, most dangerous part of London to play online video games all night. I've already thwarted several attempted muggings; partially because the English accent is fairly comical and wimpy sounding to me. I haven't been remotely scared by my would-be muggers and have been able to think quickly enough to get out of it.

CHAPTER 11

I'm still in London. I have a little time on my hands, and I wanted to share some thoughts. Unfortunately, religious extremism seems to bring out the worst in people. Suicide bombings? Who the fuck devised this as a military strategy? Wylie Coyote? I can't imagine a rational person signing up for this. "Akmed, baby, the dental plan looks phenomenal! It's just that I noticed here in the fine print that you want me to blow myself up. That is kind of a deal-breaker."

BBC runs all the old "who done it" shows like Murder She Wrote, a formulaic series with a brainy, little old lady who solves murder mysteries. Unfortunately, I think there is something much darker at play. Consider this: Jessica Fletcher is a sociopathic serial killer. Every time this geriatric "author" steps into a town, somebody gets horrifically murdered. After hundreds of bodies have turned up, it starts seeming like more than a mere coincidence. My theory is that she shows up in some small town then immediately finds a bigshot that everybody hates and murders them (to satisfy her bloodlust). Next, she picks a mark, plants a bunch of clues that only she can find; then frames the mark, makes up some elaborate story, and gets away with it every time! It is the same plot as *Basic Instinct*—if you can imagine Angela

Lansbury riding cowgirl to full orgasm, wearing a blindfold with an icepick hidden behind her back.

Speaking of things nobody wants to see, pirated DVD's are absolutely out of control in London. My former roommate, Alex, had worse taste in movies than Jay. When you think poor acting, lame cinematography, bad storyline, and just generally unwatchable; Jay's seen it. Alex has gone one step further by purchasing bootleg copies of some of the worst films ever produced off a vendor's blanket in the subway terminal. This adds an additional layer of awful to the experience. For example, *Bad Boyz 2*.

Burnett and Lowery, like Jessica Fletcher, are homicidal maniacs who think they are above the law. As the plot becomes almost instantly soulless, convoluted, and nonsensical, you can see the effects on the crowded theater. The last hour of the movie, the picture kept blacking out from the droves of people leaving the movie and standing in front of the camera, which was filming the DVD of the movie that I was watching. Pound-for-pound, it was the worst thing I have almost sat entirely through.

As I mentioned, I live in a rather international apartment. So far, I've lived with six French people, three Australians, one Spaniard, one Italian, one Albanian (I think), Dustin (I believe he is an Irish Jew,) and a Polish guy, Majik, who makes it a little easier to keep track of the grandmother land. Poland is occupying part of Iraq. This is the first occupation in Polish history, and also the creation of the first-ever Polish uniforms for desert combat.

I still work at the pub. It can be fun from time to time. I've started whistling when I'm bored; it helps to keep drunk, old British men from talking to me. My favorites include "Whistle While You Work" by the seven dwarves and "Jingle Bells." I mix it up, though. When there is a girl under the age of 65 around, I whistle "Strangers in the Night". And when we are closing the pub, I usually present my personal melody of lullabies. The other day, a customer said to me (she was Italian) "That song you make. It touches my eardrum like hundreds of little snowflakes. Each note you make is unique, is beautiful but is cold because I cannot hold on to it forever."

I have been listening to a lot of piano music and reading books…mostly the novels from the book reports I plagiarized during middle school and high school. I'm on the long, hard road to becoming sophisticated, but considering how often the path is blocked by my references to farting and masturbation, I still have a long way to go. Currently, in music, Erik Satire's "Trios Gypomnopedis" is my imaginary girlfriend's favorite song. By the way, who would have thought a superficial bastard like me would be dating an imaginary woman who had a cleft lip? What can I say? Love is blind. In the world of books, I finally read *Even Cowgirls Get the Blues* by Tom Robbin, after it sat on my nightstand for two and a half years.

Hyde Park is probably one of the best things about London, next to the weather. Hyde Park is similar to Central Park in New York. It has fresh air and a general nature which encourages maximum frolicking. If you're looking for me, I am the only twenty-three-year-old man standing alone in Hyde Park with a dead stare in his eyes, flying a two-dollar, solid black kite with a single, black streamer.

By mentioning my age, I was reminded of the next chapter of the Jam: *Jammy Jamm 5: Jack's Parties Blow*. I figure the title is fitting because it will be in the format of a Dean Martin Celebrity Roast. The roast will be followed by the reading of my last will and my brisk suicide because the only people who came to my stupid Dean Martin-style Celebrity Roast were my imaginary girlfriend (who keeps accusing me of thinking up other women), my five dachshunds, and my grandmother, who will be in the house watching an episode of *Murder She Wrote* with the volume turned all the way up to block out all the barking dogs..

PART IV: 2002
CHAPTER 12

I graduated from Florida State, and now I'm in Mexico. ¿Arriba? The flight down was going well until I became a little skeptical about our plane, thanks to our Captain's pre-landing speech.

"This is your Captain speaking," he said. "We are going to be arriving in about twenty minutes. I'm going to ask you to secure your tray tables and place your seats in the upright position. Today, we are expecting to have a rather choppy descent, so I'm just going to turn those annoying non-smoking signs off. So, feel free to light those up! Ashtrays can be found in your arm rests. Also, after this plane's last water landing, people didn't return all their flotation devices. So, for those of you without a life vest under your seat, we have placed a copy of the Gideon Bible written in Spanish. It's currently seventy degrees in Mexico City. Thank you for flying with us."

I'm staying with Fadi and Nathalie (from London) in Guanajuato, which is four hours north of Mexico City. The site of *Once Upon a Time in Mexico*, it is the most Mexican-looking place I have ever seen. I saw a ferocious Chihuahua.

Honestly, the dogs in Mexico are like monsters you see in comic books. The neighbor's dog looks like a half-German Shepard, half-wolf, which is basically a werewolf. Fadi told me, "You may find yourself surrounded by big growling dogs, but you must not be afraid. They can sense your fear." So, I'm mentally preparing myself to gouge one of these beast dog's eyes out while fending off an attack.

Niko, Fadi, and I hitchhiked north from Guanajuato, to Aguascalientes for a fiesta last weekend, as if I weren't living in a thin cocoon of fear since I got off the plane. I really wasn't thrilled about hitchhiking through Mexico, but it was one hell of an experience. I'm glad I didn't end up giving a Mexican truck driver a handjob with a gun to my face, as I initially feared, standing on the side of the Mexican interstate. Aguascalientes was fantastic, but the closest I got to picking up a girl was when I accidentally knocked over a stroller.

The language has been a small obstacle considering I am staying with eight French people who are always speaking French, and when we are in public everyone speaks Spanish. Fifty percent of my day, I play chess with the various people I have met here. We usually get a good-sized Perudo game going at night. The rest of the time, I eat, nap, and listen to people speak in different languages.

I'm enjoying the Mexican culture and food. It's a dynamic clash of conservative Catholic values with ancient Native American beliefs, relative poverty, and a strong sense of community. I can tell you from what I have seen, it isn't easy being Mexican; but it isn't easy having everyone hate your country, either.

Basically, speaking no Spanish and looking white as fuck, I give myself an eighty-three percent chance of living through this unharmed. I have noticed that the most terrifying Mexicans I've met so far drink straight tequila and smoke cigarettes. Hopefully, the fact that I'm buying shots and tossing out cigarettes like lollipops at a doctor's office will help me avert being tossed into a shallow grave in the desert.

The third most dangerous thing about Mexico after the wild, man-eating dogs and the criminal, American-hating cartels is the cholesterol. Apparently, fried dough doesn't have a serving size here, because these donuts look like rubber dodgeballs filled with custard. I can get three hot dogs for a dollar, and the pot they deep fry them in is a tar pit.

Mexico has small markets and supermarkets just like the U.S. While I can't do anything in Spanish, I can navigate an American-style supermarket like a Conquistador. The setup is almost identical to a K-mart or Target: great prices, convenience, security guards with sub-machine guns…Honestly, these guys are dressed like henchmen from a James Bond movie. One had a grenade! I just can't imagine what is going happen in a supermarket to warrant some Mexican rent-a-cop opening fire with a machine gun. My best guess is that this reasonable amount of firepower is in case one of those starving, Great Dane-coyotes breaks down a door and has to be pumped full of lead and shrapnel before it makes off with a child.

CHAPTER 13

I've been west. It was fantastic. After Mexico, I spent a week in Phoenix (Arizona) with my family. I was there for my cousin, Alex's, high school graduation. Then, I took a week of vacation in L.A. to visit some friends from high school and college. Knowing I would have to get a job soon, I spent most of my time on a four-dollar pool float sipping on Pabst Blue Ribbon and working on my fifty-five-dollar tan.

I left L.A. for Australia, which was a serious flight; sixteen hours. I performed my usual ritual of praying to Jesus to put me in the seat next to the best-looking single girl on the plane. When I boarded the aircraft, I was the only person in my row and twenty minutes later, when I heard the airplane engine start, I was still the only person sitting in my row. For the record, on a sixteen-hour flight, sitting next to no one is better than sitting next to the hottest of women.

Now, I'm living in Manly, Australia, which is just across the harbor from Sydney. I'm staying with Dillon, Grant, and Jenny. I wash dishes at Fusions, a restaurant owned by our friends, Fen-o and Emma. Also, I'm now a certified construction worker. I start my first job, tomorrow. I've been practicing my sleazy cat call. Here's what I've got so far: "Eyyy! You Aussie hookers! Come get some of this American dick! Bada-bing!"

In case anyone is wondering about my love life, I don't have one. Toby and her band, Code Red, came out with their first CD. The song "Permission" (Track 18) is written about how she and I met a couple years back. The original name of the song was, "Jack Tried to Hook-up with Me, but I'm a Lesbian: Let's be Friends." Later, she shortened the title for the album. I wrote a short story about the incident, myself.

Since I just skipped summer and went right back to winter by moving to Australia in August, I decided to hold out and wear sandals as long as possible. I now have a cold.

CHAPTER 14

After your first five shovels of dirt at 7:30 A.M., your arms tell you that construction work might not be for all people. When you have shoulders like Gwyneth Paltrow's (like me), it may be exactly what the doctor ordered. I wake up at 5:21 A.M., get to work by 7:05, and get home at 4:30. I'm usually in a bit of pain when I get home, so I take a forty-minute bath after work.

It is safe to say I've been a construction worker my entire life and I just found out. First, the weather is perfect for working outside (fifties and sixties). I get off at 3:30 every day. I get paid twenty dollars an hour and double on the weekends, which is a lot considering I do things like shovel, move rocks, and sweep. There are no customers to deal with, and most of the conversations are about women, hydraulic machinery, and horrific construction accidents involving hydraulic machinery, which, coincidentally, are my three favorite topics of conversation.

I don't have to shave, I use every curse word I can think of, and I can smoke on the job. In fact, these guys smoke on the job like there is some sort of tax rebate for it. Convenience stores sell thirty-packs of cigarettes, and if you plan on keeping up with one of these guys you are going to need at least two "magazines" if you plan on going back to the "yard" for beers after work. Basically, while hanging out at the yard you'll find the same rhetoric as being at work, but everyone is sitting down, and they're pounding beers around a burning oil drum filled with various construction materials, trash, and wood. It's right up my alley.

For many years, I've been wearing a rust-colored, leather welder's jacket that my friends got me for my birthday. It's been my most complimented article of clothing ever, and since losing my less-nice jacket, I've been wearing the leather one on the job site. The thing is, it's a man's jacket. The jacket is made to protect a welder's skin from burning, red flecks of metal, not some Nancy hipster like me who picked it out at a vintage clothing store. Often, I'll be on a job site, and an Aussie will come up to me and say, "Oi! Beautiful Jacket. Where'd ya get it? Ya done some welding 'ave ya? Fosters?" I just stare them dead in the eyes and shake my head "no," like I killed someone for it.

The animals here are pretty out of control, which is synonymous with the term "wildlife." I ran into one of Australia's most deadly spiders while at work: the Funnel Web. His venom was no match for my shovel!

At home, we have been watching some of the Olympics. I saw an ad for McDonald's, which blew my mind. No big surprise the commercial starred Ronald, acting the fool with his giant, red afro. He was "hamming it up" as an Olympic weightlifter, trying to sell your children his cheeseburgers, like he does. Then, all of a sudden, they flashed his name and nationality on the screen. Ronald McDonald: Australian. I was fucking shocked, but then it all made sense. All this time, I thought he was a clown. Now, I realize he's just from Australia.

I think Christians should modify the old Eucharist to something more progressive and delicious like sausage rolls. They are essentially a sausage stuffing packed into a warm, flakey croissant. The case is made…your move, Pope.

I tried to learn how to drive stick…again; this time, on

the left side of the road because I'm in Australia. The result was the same. After almost causing five thousand dollars in car accidents in five minutes, my instructor never mentioned teaching me again.

PART V: 2003
CHAPTER 15

I could very easily say Daytona Beach sucks, but I think you would all misunderstand me. Daytona Beach rocks, as far as finding a place to rot away and die. What sucks is the bureaucracy involved with finding a real job. What sucks even more than that is trying to find a woman. As far as needing a blow job, I've passed DEFCON ONE and have entered into EMERGCON. Honestly, if anybody knows some free porn sites, tell me. I've taken it to the limit, as far as my resources go. Hell, if you have porn, just email it to me.

Well, besides playing with myself, I'm knee-deep in a new set of paintings. Although, I feel the canvases are probably worth more money before I paint on them. I'm also finally coming around the bend on the first draft of *Painting in the Dark*, my first screenplay, also known as the never-ending nightmare that consumes my thoughts day and night. To me, writing a screenplay is like locking yourself in a cage with a cow, a hibachi, and a set of brass knuckles, and not being allowed out of the cage until you have a steak dinner for two; medium-well.

I'm also taking a Real Estate class so I can pick up some extra cash swindling old people on the weekends. Let me tell you about my Real Estate class. My school is called The Bob Fritze School of Real Estate. The school consists of an office unit with fifteen cafeteria tables and chairs to seat forty people in rows, a front podium, and a small table with a coffee maker by the front door, which is in the back of the classroom.

I sit in the very last row in the back corner with a cup of coffee and a five-dollar calculator. Bob Fritze is in his early sixties with thin, silver, combed-back hair and glasses. He teaches by telling us to highlight key passages in the book, and then communicates an explanation of the jargon with an epic personal narrative from his own life that relates to the topic.

Coincidently, his stories share the common theme that he, Bob Fritze, is the only begotten son of Real Estate, as well as the most powerful and well-connected man in Florida. Bob implies that, when it comes to "the game," he is a cunning rainmaker with a silver tongue, burdened only by a divine code of ethics and unshakeable morality. My view is that if he were half as good at selling Real Estate as he implies, he'd be on a yacht in the Caribbean, not teaching eight hours a day wearing a poorly-knotted Mickey Mouse tie, but that's my opinion. Outside of the school, I've heard Bob Fritze described as a "two-bit slum lord."

I have respect for Bob, though, on some levels; unlike the three jokers who sit to my left. To my immediate left is "Mouth;" early forties, shorts, dock shoes, no socks. "Mouth" has no concept of how loud his voice is or how to adjust it when speaking to the person next to him. Sometimes, the person seated next to him is me. When he talks, it's like he has a megaphone lodged in his throat. Every annoying sentence that he speaks is punctuated on both ends with a hyper-loud laugh, for no apparent reason.

Next down the line is "Twit." She is from Minnesota and had never seen a black person "in real life," before moving to Daytona Beach. Finally, at the end of the table is the "Waitress," whom, I suspect, was hot...ten years, sixty pounds, and two kids ago. The reason I think she was attractive is that she seems to expect attention from people, despite apparently being past the point of being able to get through life on looks alone. She is sweet as frosting but stupid as fuck. A grown woman shouldn't exclaim, "Wow!" after correctly multiplying two numbers on a pocket calculator.

So, I sit there as Bob somehow relates finding the potential gross income of property with a story about his direct conversations with God the Father. Forty minutes later, he wraps up his story by using a fire extinguisher on the burning hedge he has been taking scripture from. While the class sits in silence and disbelief, he remembers the root of his tangent and starts walking everyone through the math involved with finding potential gross income.

To my left, I don't know if it is that "Mouth" doesn't understand the concept of a rhetorical question, or if his voice is so ridiculously loud that even his head can't contain it, and he must verbalize every thought to keep from having a stroke. I usually must restrain my hand from no-look-passing my cup of coffee into his eyes, just to halt his boisterous mumblings. The worst is when the "Waitress" chimes in to make it clear that she has no fucking clue what is going on. It makes me want to stand up and Frisbee-toss my calculator across the table into her teeth; not directly for being an idiot, but more for the reason that she has created an opportunity for "Mouth" to try and talk/yell her through the problem. It's like listening to a leaf blower with a stethoscope.

Meanwhile, Bob has moved on and is trying to relate the time he held his breath for nine minutes to rescue a pregnant woman stuck in a submerged car, to estimating the reproduction cost of a garage, and he has to keep stopping to ask "the class" to be quiet. I just subtly shake my head. I know that I should just move seats, but "Twit" is cute, and I'd need to butter her up to be my alibi for when I kill "Mouth."

Speaking of death, I put Snert, one of the dachshunds, to sleep the other day. I bought him a Junior Bacon Cheeseburger from Wendy's on the way to the vet. The music selection was tricky on the ride to "the big sleep." I wasn't sure what music goes with driving your unknowing passenger to his certain death. I chose something from *The Godfather*. Later, I drank a quart of OE in mourning of my dawg.

CHAPTER 16

Well, it's official; I'm a candidate in the November 2003 election for Daytona Beach City Commissioner, Zone 1. By this time next year, with solid campaigning and some wheeling and dealing with the Prince of Darkness, I could be an overpaid political puppet. I'm tossing around some slogans: "No strong-arm is too weak for Jack." "Every man's got a price, and Jack's is consistently fifteen-to-thirty-five-percent less." Or "What do you want from me? I'm Drunk."

Well, it is also official, while waiting to be cleared to take my state real estate exam, I've had to get a job in a hotel. About the hotel, the Owner/Manager is a 5-foot Indian man named Sam. A toad-like man, his favorite phrase is "How come this?!" followed by feverishly pointing at a computer, a telephone, a microwave, or my hand puppet, "Stretch," which I crafted from a magnum condom.

I work with two very cute blondes: Ashley, who wears so much jewelry that when light hits her, she reflects like a disco ball; and Alex, who talks so fast you can hear her voice box changing gears to keep her throat from exploding. The only thing Alex loves is complaining; she hates everything about anything. She also isn't very good at her job, so her company is uniquely painful. It's a shame, because if I took her on a date…well, I can't even write about what I'd do because it's too humiliating. Just kidding. I imagine it going something like this:

First, I'd spend a ton of money on her. Money I didn't even have. Credit cards, travelers' checks, security bonds, whatever I could get. I'd probably stop to pawn my watch during the date. At dinner, we'd listen to her talk about herself, about how she wants to be a singer but has never taken lessons. She would make it clear that nothing about me even warranted a question by only allowing enough time for me to agree with her so she could continue talking, knowing that she had my attention.

Then, her phone would ring, and she'd answer it, then talk for fifteen minutes about herself, and ask me to drop her off at some guy's house because she's tired. While I'm driving, she will put on the most annoying pop station she can find, with a song I've never heard. Next, she'll start singing to my windshield before talking about herself some more. This is the point where I'd think about swerving my car into oncoming traffic in an attempt to kill us both, but since I'm a schmuck, I'll grin and drop her off. She would tell me how sorry she felt as she got out of the car. Then, some naked guy would come out of nowhere, like Sliver, and fuck her against the passenger window of my car while I sit there and wait for them to finish, so I can back out.

Back to the hotel. I was trained by a creature called Willie. Willie is a six-foot-seven black man with a slightly hunched back. He lives in what I call Willie-Time. He walks slowly, turns his head to talk slowly, he even chews his food slowly. If Willie were counting to ten out loud, it would take him sixty seconds, and the man has apparently never won a game of slaps in his life. What Willie lacks in speed, he makes up for in style. Willie has half an afro which segments his front and back bald spots like a fuzzy, dark rainbow. The first day I worked with him, he was wearing a short-sleeved collared shirt with a green polyester tie that was half a foot wide and about seven inches too short, and a stressed belt that was falling apart holding up his gray marching band pants that had red stripes down the side of each leg. Of course, these pants were too short, and the cuffs only grazed the tops of his dirty, white 1985 Reebok high-tops. He's a nice guy, though, and surprisingly misunderstood.

I went to Epcot, recently. For those of you who've never been, they have a "World Village," where twelve countries are represented in micro-Disney fashion. It's funny how it actually mirrors the world we live in. There was a band of Republicans outside France calling for a boycott; they were holding up signs that read "Freedom Fries!" Morocco added a disappointing ride called "The Opium Den" which is just a bunch of broken animatronic puppets placed on mats in a poorly lit room. Mexico and China were selling knock-off versions of all the other countries' souvenirs. Africa, unlike the other represented regions, consisted of plastic trees bellowing tribal music, a Coca-Cola hut, and a seventy-five percent higher AIDs rate than anywhere else in Epcot. I had an excellent time, considering I was the loneliest, most pathetic man in the park.

Other notables: my mother took a new job in Cape Coral, Florida. She is in the process of moving there with my grandmother and the remaining dachshunds, leaving me to care and pay for the house along with some roommates; namely, fucking Barry and one other person to be named later. While we were packing up the house, I had a chance to ask my mom why she left her job of twenty years. "Hey, Mom, so why did you choose to resign from your job so seemingly close to retirement?" I asked.

"Who are you? Fucking Dan Rather?" she replied. "Shut-up and bring this box down to the garage. And make sure Speedy doesn't get out."

"I just want to be loved," I mumbled under my breath, carrying the box.

On a personal note: my scripts suck, but I still write; my art is crap, but I still paint; and my worthless website will be back up next month, even though nobody cares.

CHAPTER 17

Rodney Dangerfield often complained about not getting respect. I'm curious if when I'm asleep, dreaming, and can't convince the girl I'm dreaming about—a figment of my imagination—to have sex with me, is that considered "no respect" or "no self-respect"?

Basically, the last time my room smelled like sex was when I masturbated while I had a fever. Technically, the only time my room has had action, I wasn't home. Speaking of my brother, Joey has been cast in a reality television show for competitive eaters. By my calculations, this should result in him getting laid even more than he does now. Considering the current ratio between our sex lives is equivalent to that of ordinary people to individuals with a third arm growing out of the center of their fucking chest, I wish him the best. They start filming in a couple months.

Other news: I'm still working at the hotel. All the good-looking girls quit, and I have so much pubic hair that when I unzip my fly, it falls out onto the floor in a mop like *Rapunzel*.

I had to go to the hospital recently for minor electrical burns after I fell asleep crying on the computer keyboard at work. I was diagnosed as pathetic, my doctor prescribed me *Chicken Soup for The Little Girl's Soul*, and then I was released the same day.

So, like I said, all the attractive girls I work with have left. Enter Allison. Allison is six feet tall and visibly overweight. Honestly, her looks are not the issue. The point is when you are built like Frankenstein's monster and have a neck like Jabba the Hut, trying to act cute to cover up your stupidity (and general incompetence) is gross. Historically, being funny, professional, sophisticated, or intelligent are all great social alternatives to healthy eating and exercise.

For example, I was standing behind the front desk wearing a white shirt, gray tie, and gray pants. Allison was in a red blouse and black work pants that need some serious tailoring, trying to make small talk. "I bet you're really sarcastic," she said. "I'm super sarcastic. We have that in common." I stared at her, expressionless. She giggled to herself and continued, "Oh my god, I love the radio station we listen to here!" She paused, "See, I was being sarcastic! Tee-hee." I continued to stare, still expressionless. She continued, "You know the people we call when we need help with our computers? I've called so many times that I have gotten to know the guy who helps, personally. His name is Ted. We can talk for hours. Have you ever done that? You know, talked to someone so much that you form this incredible bond with them?" I continued to stare at her then finally shook my head and calmly said, "No." Then, I turned my attention to the wall clock and stared, longingly.

I finished the rough draft of my first script. The working title is *Painting in the Dark*. After a couple more years of work, I might be able to sell all of the rights to it for a Nachos Bell Grande at Taco Bell. I'm excited.

CHAPTER 18

Well, after only two months, Pam, our sparky, blonde roommate, has moved out. She wouldn't give a reason for leaving, but if I were playing detective, I would place her decision somewhere between Barry sleeping on the living room couch nude, or him constantly asking if she wanted to shower together. Or it was the day Pam was walking through my room to do her laundry and saw me in bed with Molly.

"Molly" is a photo of Pam that I blew-up to life size, printed out, then cut-and-scotch taped together. I keep it under the covers next to me when I sleep, with her paper head resting on the pillow. Anyway, Pam was not impressed, nor comfortable, with Molly. She moved out the next day. Now, T.J. is moving in.

I've grown another mustache, which is an instantly regrettable decision. There is a guilty pleasure in wearing one. Unfortunately, it looks terrible. The most flattering compliment I could get would be someone telling me I look like Todd from *Boogie Nights*. I'm guessing that the mustache, at best, decreases my chances of picking up any woman by at least sixty percent, and snagging a sensible one to eighty-five. Considering my sex life is a stale illusion perpetuated between my hand and the internet, the fact that I would do anything to decrease my chances with women by willingly growing a mustache is a conundrum. I twist my bristly whiskers discreetly in the sober reflection of my decision.

I don't know how to butter up this next comment. Let's just say, this has been a long time coming. If you put more than one exclamation mark at the end of a sentence, I hate you. It's simple. The exclamation mark overage is directly proportional in exponential terms to how much contempt I have for you. If you're sitting there thinking, "Hey!!!! I do that. Does Jack hate me?" The answer is yes.

So, with all that said, it is easy to understand why I've started pricing escorts. Three hundred dollars an hour was the most reasonable one that I could find. This, to me, isn't very reasonable. Since I can't afford it, this is how I imagine my date with an escort playing out:

She arrives at the house around 9:00 pm, wearing a ton of makeup and a short, trashy looking dress. I have a mustache. Barry doesn't move from the couch where he's lying, naked, under one of my blankets, watching re-runs of Doctor Phil.

I make a pun about "escorting" her to the dining room. She smiles at me like I'm paying her to be there. We sit at the candlelit dining room table. I serve a five-course meal: red wine, a tossed salad, pan-seared tuna, lobster ravioli.

About forty-five minutes goes by. I think I'm in love. "Angel" is doing all the talking. She is telling me about the pitfalls of the modeling world while I give her a foot massage under the table.

Meanwhile, I notice a man in a ski mask creep in the unlocked front door; he has a gun. The man sneaks up behind Barry. I say nothing. He shoots Barry twice in the head. I'm overcome with joy. I run over to thank him. He mechanically turns the gun on me and shoots me in the stomach. I decided it's best to stop celebrating and head back to the dining room.

He shoots three times at Angel. She dodges two bullets and deflects a third by using the frying pan from the seared tuna. I lay on the cold kitchen floor, bleeding to death, looking up in shock over Angel's bullet-dodging antics, while the assassin stands behind me reloading his gun. We didn't even make it to dessert. Therefore, I've decided to invest my "escort money" in capital improvements for the house.

Work is absurd. The owner/manager will probably have a heart attack before the summer is over. Mom and grandma are happy. Mom is redoing the kitchen in her new house. I know she has removed a wall. I'm not sure if it is an exterior or an interior one. My brother's "reality" show, *The Competitive Eater's Ultimate Road Trip*, airs Saturday on CBS at 2 pm.

I've failed the state real-estate exam twice. I'm taking it again on Wednesday, and I should be studying right now. I'm selling the 2003 paintings as two sets. If you're interested, let me know. I'm still running for city commissioner. I bought a guitar and have begun to make the transition from poet to singer/songwriter, which is a relief because poets get as much respect as mimes, but I should really be studying real estate instead of working on my transition.

Finally, as far as *J&B's BYO-Beef & Bottle BBQ: Meet-us-the-Fetus, Farewell-to-the-Genius, and Welcoming-of-the-Guy-with-the-Same-Birthday-as-Jesus House Warming Extravaganza!* is coming—the party seems to actually be gathering momentum. This is unheard of for a party that I'm helping to throw. It's especially unique, considering its ridiculously over-the-top title.

CHAPTER 19

I passed my third Real Estate exam. The final steps are locating a broker and getting on the same page with The Board of Realtors. At the Realtor's office, I met Grace, the receptionist, an elderly lady approaching retirement. She told me I would have to pay a thousand dollars in realtor dues to work for a broker. I responded with the dark, masochistic laugh of a man with a negative net worth. I then asked if I could just pay my dues "the old-fashioned way" of getting the fucking shit kicked out of me in the parking lot. Grace was not amused.

Work is ridiculous, per the usual. Sam, the Owner/Manager, has shipped in his cousin, Ricky, from India, to maintain a proper amount of grossly incompetent people on staff. Ricky is an excitable little Indian man with the English vocabulary of an eleven-year-old. His hair is dark, straight, and combed like a choir boy's. He has a massive, black mustache that seems to cover his nostrils completely. He walks funny and he repeats himself, but personally, I don't have any real problems with him. I see myself as cordial to work with, but I wouldn't say I'm an overly affectionate person.

The other night, he caught me outside on break. He had

gone to the beach that day and was thrilled about all the girls in their bikinis. He made it expressly clear that he thought we should "cruise" the beach with his video camera. Under the circumstances, I said, "Now that sounds like an idea." What I meant to say was, "Now, that sounds like a fucking horrible idea."

I mean, honestly, I don't "cruise" the beach. I have a green 2000 Mazda Protégé that still has most of the hubcaps. My CD player is broken, and I have factory speakers; all that I listen to is public radio. Don't get me wrong, I enjoy the inconspicuousness of my car, but trying to cruise the beach with it as a tool to meet women is not a winning plan.

Furthermore, by adding a 5'4" Indian man wearing a crewneck shirt tucked into his sweatpants, hanging out my window with a giant VHS camcorder, makes the whole adventure that much more unlikely. If I wanted to be embarrassed by sailing down the beach in a piece of crap car with a douchebag hanging out the window humiliating me, I would go to the beach with Barry in his car.

I love the *A-Team*: B.A. (Mr. T), Face, Hannibal, Murdock. This was a series where every show had a super-explosive finale that was a staple of 80's action entertainment. For the *A-Team*, this weekly showdown would always serve as a testimonial to their grit, ingenuity, and rigorous training.

After watching the show for the first time in years, I couldn't help but wonder to myself: who the hell trained that band of fucking assholes? Let me recap the final seven minutes of the episode that I watched. The *A-Team* is outnumbered in a brief stand-off with a hillbilly militia of sorts. When hell breaks loose, B.A. and Face start by firing their weapons—the largest and most deadly machine guns—everywhere, apparently trying to see who could fire the most bullets without killing or wounding a human. Hannibal, with a cigar between his teeth, was literally talking in one direction and firing his weapon in another, which seems wholly irresponsible. Murdock was running around in a flowered Hawaiian shirt blowing shit up for no tactical reason: windows, cars, stacks of empty boxes.

The initial engagement lasted about four to five minutes. In this time, the *A-Team*, the elite of the elite, doesn't record one dead or wounded enemy. If it weren't for falling metal pipes and smoke inhalation, these jokers wouldn't have even won the battle. Plus, these guys are fucking mercenaries; they can't afford to spend ten thousand dollars' worth of ammunition to neutralize a dozen drunk rednecks!

Finally, as the tide turns in the favor of the *A-Team* and as the last of the enemies try to escape in a military transport vehicle, we really witness the crown jewel, a by-the-book, hostile takedown. Face, standing on a lookout tower, apparently frustrated by his lack of marksmanship, throws his gun away, then jumps four stories onto the top of a moving truck, pretending that the jump didn't break his legs. Then, he crawls to the roof on the driver's side before he swings down alongside the cab. With his free hand, he punches the driver unconscious and takes control of the vehicle. Sure, that is one way to get it done…if you were trained by the fucking *Pirates of The Caribbean*. Unlike the intro would have you believe, I now am convinced the *A-Team* was actually imprisoned in an insane asylum for impersonating soldiers.

Other than that, I still haven't drafted an editorial letter to the local newspaper with regards to my candidacy for City Commissioner. I did, however, attend my first city commission meeting, which was both awful and fascinating. My screenplays, *Painting in the Dark* and *Memoirs of a Drunk*, are almost done. I pray I can finish them within the next couple months and make some headway in that area of "Things to Do before I Die/Kill Myself."

CHAPTER 20

I recently tried to sell my soul to the devil, which was downright discouraging because he responded to my proposition by pointing and laughing at me. "I can't wait to see the look on your face," he said, then stole my spicy chicken sandwich and disappeared. I didn't read too much into it, but apparently, my Ferrari 430 Spider will have to wait.

I kept getting jobs at other hotels to leverage a higher wage at work. Well, that bold move came back to me when I was laid off at the Comfort Suites in favor of someone they could pay less to do the same job. Well played, toad man. It's not really a big deal, but the fact of my expendability did bruise my pride a bit. I've started the campaign trail for Daytona Beach City Commission Zone 1 '03. Vote for Jack Chestnut: The Name You Trust. I've learned a lot about my constituents. (1) Most of them have snarling attack dogs. (2) They don't like each other. (3) They all think I'm a salesman.

There is a slight drawback to my door-to-door campaign: I live in Florida, and it is summer. It is so ridiculously freaking hot outside that you wouldn't believe it. Two weeks ago, I was walking by a house, and it was so hot outside that the house just burst into flames. Luckily, one of the daily five-minute monsoons quickly swept over and doused the fire. If you've never lived in Florida during the summer, it's kind of like walking out of your house and being pelted with hot, wet dish rags. As if being instantly covered with sweat in the fifteen feet between your front door and the car isn't bad enough, the act of getting into your vehicle is like jumping into the fiery bowels of a pre-heated oven. It's not an atmosphere; it's living in hot chicken soup.

Since my departing from the Comfort Suites, I had to act quickly, so I charged my realtors' dues on a green credit card, found a broker, and filed for welfare. I am now a bonafide Real Estate Sales Associate with Dee's Realty, and if you can't help saying "dees nuts," I don't blame you. If you have any Real Estate needs in Florida, get in touch.

Also, since leaving the hotel, I've gotten a job as a part-time Social Studies Teacher at a Catholic middle school. They asked me if I was Catholic, I said, "Hell yes, I'm Catholic! Me and Jesus are like this!" Then I crossed my fingers and waved them back and forth in a reassuring gesture. Surprisingly, I still got the job. I start at the end of August. I'm sure I'll have a couple stories about that, soon enough.

Since I'm broke and on welfare for the next month or two, I have all my paintings on display/auction at a local Irish dive bar called Tir Na Nog (I have no idea what the name means.) It would really mean a lot to me if some of you would bid on them. I have about sixteen for sale. I'm trying to raise twelve hundred dollars. This means, when the total bids between the sixteen paintings equal twelve hundred dollars, I'll sell all the paintings to the highest bidders regardless of the price bid. Basically, a high bid on one painting makes all subsequent pieces cheaper. I'm sure none of you care, but, Uncle Walt, Bobby the Millionaire, Tommy in the Mafia, please entertain me with a bid.

My love life is still hopeless. The most common advice I

get about meeting girls is to "be myself." I've already tried being an arrogant, condescending, pretentious, unapologetic, eccentric, and bitter asshole. It hasn't worked so well. I've gone back to the drawing board.

The additional advice has been to start working out. I've been going to the gym for about a month now. Those of you who know me realize that torturing my muscles into exhaustion is something I generally want nothing to do with. I had to face the facts. Apparently, Stephen Hawking has a better chance of winning an Iron Man Race than I do of getting a girlfriend on charisma alone. Also, a picture of my upper body can be seamlessly replaced with a photo of a malnourished orphan.

So, I enter the GYM! I am, without a doubt, the smallest man in the gym. Actually, fuck that, I am the smallest human being in the gym. I dress in the full *Cable-Guy* motif: short-shorts, headband, sweatbands, and tube socks. I've named my gym towel "Beautiful." It has a picture of me flexing in a pair of white, cotton underwear. Sometimes, I talk to it while I'm pumping iron.

I have replaced the weightlifter's grunt with exasperated profanity. "FUCK! One…Fuck this is heavy! Two…Motherfuck Errr! Three…Lift Bitches! Four…Fuck me! Five…"

The one thing that baffles me about the gym is why there are so many jacked-up, gray-haired old men in there. Why does a seventy-year-old man need enough strength to deadlift a Buick?

The other points of interest in my circus-like life include that T.J. bought a puppy. He's a German Shepard-Chow mix named Buddha; we're calling it a German Chow-pard. I still hate Barry. To prove it, I just wrote "fuck you" on all his eggs with a sharpie.

CHAPTER 21

Yes, I'm a teacher. I tried to tell a story about it, but teaching stories are generally a "you had to be there" experience. I'm sure something genuinely entertaining will happen, soon. Meanwhile, my school is having a fundraiser this Saturday and my best friend, T.J., has also gotten me two tickets to the Rolex 24 Hour Race the same night. Since I'm pathetic, I was thinking about taking out an advertisement in the newspaper:

Have you ever wondered what it would be like to be on a date with Jack Chestnut? Have you ever wondered who the fuck Jack Chestnut is? Possibly lost sleep over it? Well, for one lucky winner, your longing is over.

The date will start with Jack rescuing you from your current tower in his emerald green, surprisingly roomy, Mazda Protégé. Don't worry about gas, because Jack has plenty of it. You will arrive with the ultimate escort to "The Great Gatsby Gala" fundraiser, where you will "enjoy dinner and dancing" while bidding on all your favorite items. Zoot Suits and Flapper Dresses are welcome but not required. Just as you are wondering "Did I win dinner with Heath Ledger?" it will be time for the savory second course.

That's right. "Start your engines;" you're going to the

Rolex 24 Hour. You'll enjoy the race and fireworks from the largest Ferris wheel on the east coast. The checkered flag will wave, and you'll be wondering, "Did I just watch the greatest sports entertainment showcase in the world with Jude Law?" But before it sinks in, it's off for the breakfast of your choice from any of the local restaurants. While you're thinking, "This can't get any better," it does, because safely at your front door, you will receive a parting gift; an original Jack Chestnut painting of anything you want (except a dog).

Here's how the contest works: If only one girl responds to this, she wins. In the unlikelihood that more than one female responds, this whole plan becomes extremely complicated. If no one responds, then there is no winner, only a loser: Jack. This contest is open to any woman over the age of 21.

Speaking of paintings, I sold sixteen paintings for twelve hundred dollars. I'd like to thank my benefactors: Kentucky Gentlemen Whiskey and Camel Lights. Honestly, thank you, to the hand full of you that bought the pictures. I've done about twenty more paintings in the past two months, and I'm almost ready to sell the new work. I've decided I wanted to have a "one-man art show" as if my art were somewhere important, instead of on the side wall of a dive bar called "The Tir Na Nog," which I found out means "The Land of The Young" in Gaelic. Unfortunately, there is nothing young about the place, the linoleum floors, the low ceiling, or the tables. You name it: it's dilapidated. The cheapest way to renovate the bar would be to explode the building, which may be considered an improvement.

In media, I've recently been subjected to a Doctor Pepper commercial featuring Meatloaf's masterpiece "*I Would Do Anything for Love*." There are many things that I hate about this particular song: the words, the guitar riffs, Meatloaf's voice, post-production. I even hate the title of the album, Bat Out of Hell. Is Meatloaf the bat out of hell? If he is, I'm asking him to please return to hell and take his music back where it belongs, playing for the people who should be listening to it: the damned.

T.J.'s dog, Buddha, is doing well. He is almost big enough to kill a human. Speaking of which, Jim and I finished the first draft of *Memoirs of a Drunk*. We've decided that animating the movie is our most viable option for getting it made. So, now, I'm going to have to learn how to do animation, which is kind of a big step for me. The story is fucking hysterical and worth the effort, so I'm looking forward to starting the next steps.

Gas prices are way up, and some people are feeling the pinch. To put it in perspective, Barry said if he had a thirty-gallon truck, he would drive it up to the gas station, fill the thing with fuel, review the meter after pumping to verify that it says a hundred plus dollars, then pump two gallons of additional petrol onto his truck and himself. Finally, he would get back into the truck, scream something in Arabic, and light a cigarette. In this situation, I did volunteer to pay for the last two gallons of gas and the cigarettes.

PART VI: 2004
CHAPTER 22

I've been a Middle School teacher for almost six months without being fired. Those wacky, little bastards are always a handful. They all call me Mr. C because they can't pronounce my real last name. As promised, here is a story about teaching:

The other day, in my 8th Grade American History class, there was an incident. Enzo, a chubby, Italian thirteen-year-old had interrupted my class enough times that I had to move him to another seat. Remember, I'm losing my hair, and I haven't had sex in over a year, so I'm never in a good mood, but I try and be patient. So, I placed Enzo in a seat at the front of the class that was pressed flush against the white board—his back turned to the rest of the class.

I then continued my lesson on Alexander Hamilton and The Bank of the United States, which is a particularly arduous task because thirteen-year-olds do not give a fuck about the implications of a nationalized banking system and its effects on the individual state economies. Regardless, before I had even finished my next sentence, Enzo—the fool—had turned around to make a comment to another student sitting with the rest of the class. I was shocked. Decisively, I walked over to my desk. I took out an office referral and a piece of tape, then stuck the referral to the board in front of Enzo. I said, "Enzo, I don't have time for your shenanigans. If you want to talk, talk to this," directing his attention to the referral. Feeling I had resolved the situation, I turned my attention back to the class; then out of the corner of my eye, I saw the unthinkable. Enzo was motioning to turn his head and make another comment. I couldn't take it.

I quickly slid behind him. The base of his turning jaw nestled perfectly into the palm of my waiting right hand as he moved to say something stupid to the class. When he saw me, my left hand was already on the top of his tiny skull. I swiftly jerked my right hand in the opposite direction. The sound his neck made while it was breaking was like the crystals popping in a new glow stick. It was horrific; the screams of his classmates were justified. Enzo's head was one-hundred-eighty degrees from its natural position, his eyes were dead, and his tongue was hanging out. A bit of blood came from his nose and dripped over his lips. My hands were still shaking, pumping with adrenaline. I let go. His body went limp and fell on the desk, his lifeless face staring at the ceiling.

That's when I realized my classroom management skills were about to be put to the test. Lacy, a straight-A student, and usually very bubbly, was crying hysterically. She tried to run for the door, but I caught her with a firm clothesline that kicked her legs out from under her. She landed on her back and started gasping for air. I put my foot on her chest and walked over her.

Danny, who wanted to play basketball when he got older, made a break for the door to my left. He almost got by me, but I grabbed him by the throat and with a judo-style sling shot, sent him fifteen feet backward. The soles of his high tops grazed the heads of his ducking classmates as he crashed through the second story window and onto the pavement below.

I walked over to the broken window, stared down at his contorted body, then I yelled, "Hey, Danny! You're dismissed!" Feeling the situation was now under control, I straightened my tie and turned my attention back to Hamilton's solutions for rescuing the U.S. economy after the revolutionary war, while my students whimpered quietly at their desks.

I'm still living in Daytona Beach, Florida, working as a social studies and theology teacher at a Catholic middle school. I'm still bitter, despite having a superb life and a loving family. I still live with Barry, who, despite my typically irresistibly persuasive banter, has not yet killed himself (but I will keep trying to convince him.) I still live with T.J., who loves being the most influential/only Asian American in NASCAR. My good friend and contemporary, Jimmy, recently moved into the house after spending a couple years in L.A. I ended the second-longest sex drought of my life by having unprotected sex with a thirty-year-old ex-prostitute, so now I probably have AIDs, which in all fairness, I'd rather die of than lung cancer. Other than that, I can't buy a girlfriend, which is surprising because I'm pretty good at buying friends.

After a couple guitar lessons, I'm now claiming the birth of my music career. My writing style is a cross between Jonny Cash and Jeff Buckley. Unfortunately, my raw guitar style and limited vocal range have been described as "wasting someone's time by shitting in their ears."

I did some stand-up comedy at an open mic recently, and this is the joke that I used:

Any Star Wars fans? I watched the original Star Wars trilogy, alone, naturally. I imagined what it would be like to work for the Empire:

Imagine a Thursday, a little after lunch, on an Imperial spaceship. Tom, who works under Darth Vader, visits Human Resources (HR) about a transfer. Bill, who is the head of the department, takes the meeting in his weird looking, ultra-modern office.

"Tom, how are you? Have a seat."

"Hey, Bill. I have to get straight to the point."

"Okay, Tom, what's on your mind?"

"Well, I want a transfer. I been working for Darth Vader for about six months now, and frankly, the guy scares the shit out of me. He has no sense of humor, he's always breathing down my neck, and the other day I saw him stick his fucking hand out in mid-air and choke one the IT guys to death. Nobody said a damn word to him. You know why, Bill? Because we're all scared."

Bill adjusted his posture, as he took in the information.

"Tom," he said, "I think the problem here is clear. It sounds like you don't like black people."

CHAPTER 23

I realized my social interactions with girls are essentially like a psychological litmus test; whereas, if a girl is considering having sex with me, she is most likely already suffering from clinical depression. In other relationship news: I broke up with my imaginary girlfriend, again. She got pregnant. I told her I couldn't afford to have any more hallucinations running around my house.

It's almost summertime, here in Florida. That means all those monstrous flying insects from the tropics, AKA *The Mist*, have begun migrating to the Sunshine State for its steaming, hundred-degree, petri dish of an atmosphere. This is also known as the worst time to fall asleep drunk on the couch overnight with your porch door open and lights on.

One morning, I woke up and went downstairs to my bedroom, and it looked like something you'd see in an *Indiana Jones* movie. I ignored the fifty smaller moths eating my bed spread and fluttering around the room. I locked eyes with Eskaminzim, which means "big mouth" in Apache. This moth was the size of a hubcap, and its meaty legs were clinging to my ceiling fan blade like a surfboard it was about to paddle out on and catch a wave.

It was, hands down, the most intimidating moth I'd ever

seen. I had to do something before I left for work, and I had to do it quickly. I did my best to escort the small moths outside while I kept my eyes on Eskaminzim. I mean, a creature that formidable in size, you can't just smack with a shoe; hell, it had my slipper in its mouth. After it dropped my house shoe, the thing growled at me, which was even worse.

I didn't know what I was going to do if it flew at me. I knew that I might lose the fight. Even so, I would have to defend myself, but it wouldn't be easy. It would probably look like a scene from *Godzilla vs. Mothra*, and even if I won the battle, I was concerned about getting blood and moth wings everywhere. I knew if it came down to a matter of life or death, I would need to beat Eskaminzim with some sort of bat…maybe even stab it.

In the end, it wasn't hungry enough to attack. I tried to spare both our lives by leaving the door to the room open while I went to work. When I returned home, I was relieved to find that the beast had flown off. Unfortunately, he decided to exit by smashing through my closed window instead of using the open door. He also took my favorite pillow as a snack for the road.

Summer brings things much worse than moths, like Bike Week; a non-stop rumbling of leathery people and jackets everywhere saying sleazy things to bartenders who are dressed like they are prisoners of Jabba the Hut.

I also went to the PGA Players Championship. I was the obnoxious guy wearing dark plaid pants, double fisting beers and screaming, "Get in the hole!" when the ball was nineteen feet from the pin, and at a dead stop.

Barry's birthday party was a sausage fest. Shocker.

This is how I want to die: I'm sitting by the pool, eating lunch. I finish my stacked club sandwich and decide to go swimming in my pool—which is filled with beer instead of water. I do a lazy "can opener" off the diving board and splash into the refreshing brew. Then, I giggle at the thin layer of head that my entrance has created; it tickles. I start to laugh because I am so rich that I own a pool filled with Miller Lite. Oh no! I get a cramp. I laugh, I can't swim from the pain of the cramp, and I'm laughing so hard at the fact that I could drown in beer. My head goes under. It's delicious. I struggle to make it back to the surface for air. I break the lager and gulp some air for a change. I feel fantastic. In the end, when the police find me, they are unable to determine if it was an accident or suicide.

CHAPTER 24

Florida! Why are you so hot? It's only April! It's like getting hit with napalm every time I go out to get the mail. This is one of many reasons why I'm moving to New York, eventually. Beforehand, Dustin and I are returning to Europe to confirm that we are getting old. It's only a ten-day adventure surrounding the World Cup, but looking at history, it should be two hundred hours of mischief.

As for now, I'm coming to the end of Easter break from school. I had a pleasant vacation. As a Catholic theology teacher, I try to show proper meal ticket appreciation. For Lent this year, I went forty days without eating bacon, which was a million times harder for me than going without sex, like I did last year.

Most people know I love bacon. On a good day, all three of my meals will feature a couple strips. So, the forty days were rough; I lost my appetite, I was only eating half of my food, and I couldn't sleep. Burger King commercials were giving me cold sweats. I caught myself rubbing my face against a jar of Bacon Bits in the grocery store (cursing quietly to myself about the decision to go cold hammy). I hope you're happy, Jesus. Never again.

I spent last weekend in Miami. I was in town for my

friend, Jenny's, wedding. My friend, Alex, from the hotel, was my date. I got to Miami in the morning. Through circumstance and luck, I was able to get a hotel room that afternoon on South Beach and Alex brought four friends, which was great for my ego.

Alex and I went to the wedding around 5 P.M. It remains physically astounding to watch how much time she spends on her cell phone. She never lets it charge either, so she is basically connected to a wall outlet via her cell charger everywhere she goes—work, the gym, a friend's house, or the club. Even when we are together, if I have a question, I just send her a text message.

The wedding was perfect. I want Jenny to plan all my weddings. After the wedding, Alex, her friends, and I went back to the hotel to get changed for the clubs.

Miami's blistering heat and strong Latin American influence have created a unique fashion scene which features pretty slutty looking, microscopic clothing. I love it.

The five girls and I hit the street. Honestly, I felt like a pimp. That initial feeling was confirmed when a squad car flashed their lights at us. They then cut us off at the intersection to question us about where we were going. The officer was clearly insinuating that I was a pimp, or even possibly that I was selling my slender body as a sex toy for cash and drugs, which in retrospect, was probably the case.

Other than that, I spent the evening waltzing through the South Beach VIP scene thanks to Alex and her friends. I've found that VIP status will get you into the club without paying a cover charge. The VIP status will get you into the private room. However, when you finally get to that VIP Bar and order a VIP drink, you get VIP sodomized when you pay for it, with the realization that paying three times as much per regular drink virtually negates any benefit of being a VIP in the first place. All-in-all, even without hooking up, I had a great time.

After a heartfelt discussion with my penis, I've decided

to change my strategy with women. I give up. I'm waiting till I'm thirty, and I'm ordering a bride from the former Soviet Bloc.

Other news: Barry is my only friend, and I hate him for it. He claims that once he moves to Orlando, I will run out of negative things to say about him. I assure all of you that my hate for the Barrester is boundless. If I ever do stop writing about how much I want him to run face-first into a tether ball pole, then I have stopped out of respect for someone else and not for a lack of inspiration.

PART VII: 2005
CHAPTER 25

Here is a list of a few things I don't understand: like, if everyone has caller ID integrated into their phone, do I really still need to leave a message? What is the difference between a transsexual and a transvestite? Is there any animosity between the two groups (transsexuals, and transvestites) because of incidences of mistaken identity? I don't dare type either word into google for fear of the things I might see. Above all else, I don't understand the forty-to-sixty-year-old men I see waving their twenty-pound metal detectors over the sands of Daytona Beach like they're about to find buried treasure.

It's the worst investment I've ever seen! Honestly, what the fuck are these guys expecting to find? First, the beach is enormous! More importantly, it gets regularly raked by the city, you fucking morons! The chances of these guys finding anything of value in the sand are non-existent. On a great day of metal detecting, one guy will find two soda tabs, a pair of nail clippers, and a nickel.

Considering what he paid for his detector—or as I call it, his two-hundred-dollar trash locator package—which includes his sub-sonic earphones and sand scoop on a pole (so he doesn't have to bend over and face the humiliation of the fact that he's unearthed another foil condom wrapper,) his white orthopedic sneakers and matching tube socks, plus time and energy added up, minus the value of what he finds on the beach; the return on the investment is equal to getting punched in the face every time he picks something up. What a disgrace. I just don't understand it. Sadly, the big difference between this geriatric buffoon and me is that when he was my age, he had a sex life, but when I'm his age I'll only have the ownership of a metal detector and orthopedic shoes.

I really don't see how I'm going to get a consistent and robust piece of ass in Daytona Beach. Between my own futility, Daytona Beach, and Barry, it's really not even worth trying.

I blame myself—I take people's advice. People say, "You should just be yourself." I've been just-being-myself for years. There is now evidence that I suck. People say, "He who cares least wins." I don't care. You know what? Nobody cares that I don't care.

Then, there is me in Daytona Beach. I went out to a bar the other night. It was like The Club House from *The Little Rascals*. I was looking around for a sign that said: No Girls Allowed.

So, you have Daytona Beach and me, now add Barry. Hanging out with Barry is so much fun. It's like being at your birthday party. Everyone is singing the birthday song. The room is lit by a lamp and the candles on your cake. A flash from a camera goes off. People giggle. Everybody is having fun. The room goes quiet as you lean over to make a wish and blow out the candles. *Whoosh!* The unthinkable happens. Barry is blowing out the candles on your birthday cake. He circles around trying to get to all the candles, but he runs out of breath. He looks up at you with a shit-eating grin. You both look at the one remaining candle. Barry blows out the last candle; you're shocked, and no one is having fun anymore except Barry.

If you can imagine that much fun in a town with more

dudes than Key West and my crippled game, the likelihood that I'm going to have a girlfriend before summer is dead. The likelihood of me getting a blow job from a prostitute in Amsterdam is alive.

As some of you already know, every week, I go up to Barry's room while he is at work and take one of his socks from his drawer. I keep them in a shoebox under my bed. In total, I have a baker's dozen of his mismatched socks and one of his tennis shoes. I've decided if Barry won't simply kill himself, I'm either going to have to drive him insane and/or murder him. But murder is such an ugly word. I prefer to describe it more like a surprise.

It's really a simple plan. While Barry is not at home, I'm going to dig a six-foot deep pit in my backyard, fill it with sharpened sticks, take a shit in it, and then cover the hole with palm fronds and leaves. Then, I'll just wait it out. Surprise! You fell into a Burmese tiger trap.

About five months ago, the Florida State Seminoles played in a little game called the FedEx Orange Bowl. It was played in Jacksonville, and I was lucky enough to get some tickets. The day started off like any other great day of football. I was with my friends, Jason, Jay, and T.J., tailgating outside Jacksonville Stadium with my brother and his friends. Barry was there.

After a jovial couple hours of beer hydration in the parking lot, we made our way to the stadium. This was when I started feeling hungry, in fact, starved. First, I got one meatball sub. It was unstoppable. I got a second; it was just as good as the first. Jason couldn't finish his chicken sandwich. I ate that, too. The game started, and I was all right. I was drunk. Being able to cheer for my Seminoles again was great. The score was 14-13 at halftime. I was still hungry, and I couldn't believe it. I did something foolish: I bought another meatball sub. It didn't go down easy. In the last couple bites, I burped. That is when I knew I had made a big mistake.

The pain crept in slowly. I cheered through the third

quarter. By the fourth quarter, I couldn't stand anymore. I was sprawled out in my seat just wailing in pain, only getting updates from the action in the game that was literally taking place in front of me. I felt like my stomach was pushing against my ribs. It was excruciating. I couldn't even move my legs to let people walk by. The game went for three overtimes, and we won.

I staggered out through the parking lot to the car with Barry, Jason, and T.J. Barry, who enjoys annoying me, feels compelled to question every decision that I make. He has been right a couple times but most of the time, he is just a pain in the ass. So, he was constantly asking me about heartburn, which I didn't have. I was really in too much agony to give my usual lengthy arguments and justification to Barry for decisions I make that solely affect me. I snapped when we pulled over at a gas station. I bought milk and Barry looked at me like he was going to say something. I couldn't handle it. I yelled at him, "It's fucking science!" It was loud, it was obnoxious, it was wrong. I was in a lot of pain. I know milk is a temporary solution, with some drawbacks. I'd accidentally claimed milk was a base when it's really a weak acid. So, arguing that "it was science" makes me an idiot (but who didn't know that). It was almost useless for my problem, which wasn't really heartburn in the first place. It was the fact that I put more food in my stomach than it could comfortably hold. I was fucking thirsty for a glass of milk, and the milk made some of the pain go away immediately. I'm not sure why. It's just science to me.

The car ride home was filled with me burping and whimpering as I started to feel better. Unfortunately, the burps were so foul they could bubble the paint off a Bentley, but what mattered to me was the pain was subsiding, just like Mr. Wizard promised.

CHAPTER 26

Right now, I'm on vacation from teaching middle school. It's been two weeks since I've been in a heated argument with a twelve-year-old, which is fantastic. I'm not going to say I sped out of Daytona, but apparently, I did speed out of North Carolina and into Virginia. I was driving a lackadaisical 77 miles per hour and wasn't even sure that there was a problem until I saw the flashing lights behind me.

Gauging by the way that the officer exited his vehicle and then approached mine, I had the distinct impression he was going to write me a ticket. Mainly, it was when he stopped at my trunk and began to hump-thrust my car while pointing at me through the reflection in my rearview mirror. I could see that trying to charm my way out of this ticket was unlikely. Plan B was a little surprise that I had picked up in Jamaica. I quickly stabbed the state trooper voodoo doll I kept in the glove box with a pencil; it didn't work. The ticket was four hundred dollars.

After my guns-a-blazing entrance, I spent several days in Virginia visiting my friend Curtis, who is studying for the California Bar Exam at the University of Virginia – Charlottesville, an elegant campus designed by Thomas

Jefferson. I got there Thursday morning, had a great time Thursday night, which turned into a terrible time Friday morning, afternoon, and evening. I left Saturday. The "off" things about my days there were both my stomach and the power. Literally, it was the most power outages in a three-day span that I'd ever seen.

Day after day, everything in Curtis' apartment shut off and then turned back on all at once. Then off, (two hours later) on…off. It wasn't even fucking raining at the time. The weather was overcast with mild winds and you shouldn't have no electricity for three hours because of a breezy day.

Saturday, I drove up to New York from Virginia. I picked up Dustin, and we joined my Aunt Theta for a weekend in scenic, upstate New York. My Aunt owns a house in a little town outside of Woodstock, in the Catskill Mountains.

If Woodstock had a hospital, I would have been born in it (but hospitals aren't the only thing missing from Woodstock). Woodstock is ninety-two percent tranquil woodland paradise with light shimmering through the majestic trees. The other eight percent of Woodstock is the always malnourished, often rabid, sometimes wily grizzly bear population, which makes it a lovely place to die.

Assuming I couldn't get into the house during one of the bear raids, I've weighed my options. I could spray the charging beast with a garden hose, or I could try to outrun the four-legged predator on the rugged mountainside with tears streaming down my face. I've concluded that if I see a bear, I'm just going to jump into its mouth.

Meanwhile, Dustin and I were too horny to be concerned with bears, and it was Saturday night. Our plan was general—go out for a couple beers in the town, meet girls, possibly convince them into doing unladylike and potentially regretful things, and take a cab back to my Aunt's or get dropped off.

Due to some massive oversights in the first half of our

night, we basically had one drink in a bar that was closing, then spent the next two hours walking cluelessly for miles down an unlit road in the wrong direction, unable to make a phone call. Woodstock has plenty of bears but doesn't have any cell phone towers. As we approached the original bar, we finally saw the second bar that we'd been looking for. It was the only restaurant in Woodstock open past midnight, and it sucked.

Woodstock doesn't have taxi service on Saturday night, either. There were about twenty-five dudes there, two girls with their boyfriends, one girl working, and two other women who were members of AARP, and the pay phone was broken. This brings me to an interesting point to make about the likelihood of meeting the girl of my dreams in Woodstock.

Imagine I'm at home in Woodstock. There is a knock at my door! I don't get many visitors, and cell phones don't work. "Who is it?" I say.

"My name is Jill, I heard there was a really cute guy who lives here, and I hope you don't mind if I introduce myself."

"Hold on," I quickly unlock the door and open it. *Snap!* I've been eaten alive by one of those fucking grizzly bears. Point being, in Woodstock, you are more likely to get masticated by a giant bear than to eat a little beaver.

In the end, I was able to bribe the bartender to give us a lift the last ten miles to the house after his shift ended. Dustin went back to the city on Monday. I drove in with my aunt on Tuesday after drawing several sketches of her dogs. While in the city, I've run into several old friends: Dustin's Family, Amanda, Rich and Kellie, and Brendan, and I've had fun every night.

Saturday, for example, Brendan and I went out in the city. It was my first exposure to real hipsters. After going to several bars, Brendan and I went to a "party" which was held at a club, so it was more like we went to a club than a party. There was a line to get in, the place was called Miss Shapes. Instead of some stereotypical brute with a flashlight checking IDs, I was surprised to see a husky little white dude with skin-tight jeans down to the tapered ankle and a blue t-shirt, hand-picking people to go inside. Lucky for us, Brendan was wearing a pink sweater and we were allowed to enter after a group of guys in women's jeans and a group of ladies who looked like they were going to a comic con. I'll admit, the inside of the bar was impressively well-designed, and the music was great.

It was like a hipster playground. To gauge how "hip" you are in the scene seems to be correlated with how ridiculously uncomfortable and unnatural you look in your clothes. It was like the inter-species cantina from *Star Wars*. This description was consistent with the five 6'6" cross-dressers towering over the crowd in high heels, fifteen little Asian girls in 50's bee-bop dresses, twenty-five Sid Vicious homages, and a hundred people in-between. Brendan was seized by some girl within minutes; they made out for about half-an-hour before returning to her lair. I was just shocked that with all the shenanigans going on around me, how good the music was. I took a cab home..

CHAPTER 27

The plane flight to Amsterdam was adequate. We got the cheapest tickets we could find. Our seats were located right behind coach, known as "broken-chairs" or "no class." We fast-forwarded through time, the ocean, and the night. After just three hours of darkness, we arrived at 7:00 A.M. Dutch time.

Even without jet lag, Amsterdam can be a confusing place. Instead of the conventional grid-style system of streets, central Amsterdam's roadways form an arching amphitheater that wraps around in concentric circles radiating from the unsavory central train station. Besides making it intolerable to give directions, the continuously curving roads make it impossible to see more than fifty feet in front of you, while giving you the distinct feeling that you are always walking in circles.

Even though Dutch people often speak four languages, Dutch, itself, is completely indecipherable and devoid of hints; it feels like you are supposed to unscramble the letters, but it doesn't work. In Amsterdam and other parts of Holland, you'll find a smorgasbord of transportation alternatives. Instead of the American standard of four lanes of cars, in Amsterdam, you'll find one lane for the trolley, one bicycle lane, two lanes for cars, and sidewalks all blitzing by in harmony. Never before has crossing the road offered so many ways to be run over by something. If you make it across the street alive, you'll soon notice that the Red Light District certainly has no shortage of homeless, desperate drug addicts about every twenty feet.

First, some junky is playing a recorder for spare change. He is followed by another schmoe juggling tennis balls for spare change. That guy is followed by yet a third drug addict threatening to slit your throat with the knife in his pocket if you don't give him your spare change. This cycle is pretty standard. Take all that and add the funkiest, most powerful marijuana in the world, plus calypso music, and you'll get the pseudo-nightmarish carnival of sin that is Amsterdam's Red Light District. In other words, it's too hot to handle, too cold to hold. Since Dustin and I travel with a great deal of ambivalence, we only spent a couple hours in Amsterdam before leaving for Den Hague (The Hague).

Amsterdam is the capital, but The Hague is the center of government in the Netherlands. Den Hague is a very pleasant, well-designed city. Everyone seems very cheerful for no particular reason; kind of like the Lego people with their permanent smile...those smug, little yellow-headed bastards.

The Dutch seem to be a very modern people. Pilots take a retinal scan before being allowed to enter their terminal, toilets have two levels of flush to conserve water, and hotel key cards tell the elevator what floor you are on. Our hotel room looked like it was straight out of an Ikea catalog: two comfy beds, dark wood furniture, a 16-inch flat screen TV, two-way opening windows, and a frosted glass wall.

We wanted to watch the U.S. play Italy, so we got some suggestions on where to go. It had been a pretty long day, so far. Dustin decided to take the first shower. I sat in a chair by my bed, watched soccer, and wrote about European 900-number commercials, which are basically two minutes of pornography with a number at the bottom of the screen.

Who needs to call the number? They're giving it away! Those lucky, little European rascals! When I was a kid, I had two options: one, trying to make out titties through the scrabbled signal of an adult TV station, or watch USA's *Up All Night* for five hours waiting to see nudity, which always seemed to be one scene away, but never was. These kids get two or three channels of free 900-number porn after 11:30. It's not fair.

As I was writing, I noticed the light in the room was flickering from something behind me. I turned around. To my ultimate displeasure, I was looking at Dustin's silhouette on the other side of the frosted glass wall, naked and clueless, care-freely scrubbing his balls with a hand towel. "Oh no!" I naturally shrieked and turned away. I yelled to him, but he couldn't hear me. I only turned around once more, and that was to take a picture.

It wasn't Dustin's cholesterol that concerned me as much as the truth that more than one flower-picking Dutch pervert thought that installing a translucent bathroom wall was a good idea. If I were staying at that hotel with my eighty-seven-year-old grandmother, and that happened, I'd have to throw myself through the two-way opening window. Basically, there is one way that shower is a good idea, and thousands of ways it is a lousy idea.

Later, we went to a bar to watch the U.S. soccer team (AKA a bunch of fucking bums) tie Italy. The next day, we left Den Hague and went to Brussels, the capital of Belgium. We found a great room at a hostel, thanks to my travel agent mother. Famous for Van Damme and waffles, I truly enjoyed Brussels.

Our hostel was giving away beers for about a dollar each. The beer reminded me more of TNT. The bottles were tiny, about 10 ounces, but like TNT, they were extremely volatile. Each beer had around 9% alcohol, unlike Bud Light which is 4.2%, so we played it safe and had a little over a dozen each that night. The next morning, I woke up, and it felt like there was an explosion inside my skull—it was miserable. In the end, we decided to spend an extra night in Belgium before heading to Switzerland.

CHAPTER 28

At sunrise, Dustin and I left Belgium for Switzerland, via France. It's astonishing how many different positions there are to fall asleep in your chair while riding on a train; it's like sleepy Kama Sutra. We entered France mid-morning, which French border officers call "Frisk o'clock." They quickly slammed Dustin's face up against the train's window and started demanding to know where the drugs were. They patted me down and dumped my luggage out onto the seat. Because of reasonably accurate profiling techniques, this is basically the same reception Dustin and I get in every country. They kept demanding to know where the drugs were, and since we didn't have any, I pointed at Dustin and said, "They're up that guy's ass." Dustin was not pleased with me as they dragged him away.

We arrived in Interlaken around late afternoon. It wasn't long before we were surrounded by old friends. The next three nights are a bit blurry. I labeled them: Night one, I lost balance and fell over so many times it looked like I was on roller skates (strike one). The second night, I was drunker than the elephant man's mother. I was tongue kissing in the bar and then I tried to take a short-cut home, got lost, and was picked up by the police (strike two). The third night, I got drunk, and then I got lucky (homerun). We left the following day.

About the run-in with the police: I was lost, it was 3:30 A.M., I was rumbling, bumbling, staggering drunk; I had a pocket full of marijuana and no identification. When I saw the flashing lights, I knew it was over. I was outraged when the police officers made me get in the back seat of their car, and then drove me home to my friend's house and told me not to leave. That's it?!

I was fuming. You call that law enforcement?! What? You're not going to cuff my hands behind my back? You're not going to read me my rights? These cops are pussies. No fingerprints? No mug shots? Are you out of your minds, you candy-ass, Rolex-having chocolate lovers?! What about my $1,500 fine? How come I'm not doing twenty hours of community service picking up trash for some fat ass in a dump truck? With fresh fish like me, you have to milk it; take every penny! What about my inconvenient court date? I've seen Toys 'R' Us security guards with more aggression! I'm a dangerous man! I just committed like three misdemeanors. I'm American for fuck's sake; break out that taser! Somebody needs to tell these socialists that their brutal style of tyranny is unacceptable, and America will destroy them to directly establish real freedom and social justice without their interference.

So, Dustin and I planned this trip to watch the World Cup after a heartbreaking exit four years ago. I waited four years to see these heartless rookies get rolled over like a bunch of ballerinas at a weightlifting competition. Granted, Ghana spent more time pretending they were injured than playing soccer, and there were more shots of the stretcher being brought out than shots on goal. But that is no excuse! The totality of the team's performances was the least clutch thing I've ever seen. I take that back. Dustin in Den Hague, higher than a weather balloon, out of nowhere hurling the last two grams of hash into a drainage ditch like he was returning Excalibur to the Lady of the Lake, was the least clutch thing I've ever seen.

After a brief stay with Ken-tastic in Zurich, we made our way to Luxembourg for a night, and then finally back to Amsterdam. I felt lucky to get on the plane, considering my Three Stooges performance trying to get my things and self through security and onto the aircraft.

Since returning to the United States, I made a trip south to stay with my mother in Cape Coral, Florida for a month. On the journey down, I spent a day in Charlotte with Heather, a few days in Tallahassee with Chris and his family, and Independence Day with those rascals in Daytona Beach, before finally arriving at Camp Chestnut.

There are pros and cons to spending quality time with my mother. Pro: I eat well. Con: wheelbarrowing hundreds of pounds of hot cow shit for landscaping. Pro: I keep my grandmother company, and work on my projects. Con: my grandmother has lost her short-term memory and asks me if I'd like an ice cream cone ten to fifteen times a day. Pro: with my mother's support, I haven't smoked in a week. Con: I really want a cigarette.

I'll be moving to London after another year of teaching. I've decided to buy a dog. I'm going to name it Barry, then give it up for adoption, immediately.

THE END

The Song of
Her Sea

THE DRIVE

In an open desert,
on a sunny drive,
all run and nowhere to hide.

The past and present had arranged to collide.
His mind opened wide,
battling with a familiar tide,
thrashing through waves of memory,
as they perpetually churned inside.

HER PHOTOGRAPH

It was a sleepy Sunday
when I first saw your face
in a tiny wooden frame,
hanging on a wall
at my friend's place.

A black and white photo;
an enigma with grace.
Hypnotized and haunted by you,
paralyzed by someone new.

WISH & TELL

I wished she were mine,
fumbling through a pocket of pennies, nickels, dimes.
Wasting time, watching my token dreams as they splash
and shine in the sea, below.
Nowhere to go,
on a rainy, Tuesday afternoon.
To this parking lot puddle
over which I huddle,
I ask if history mentions my struggle.
Let it tell that you were a piece of that puzzle,
and not a little, watery grave.

THE ECLIPSE

The lime irises of her eyes
seemed in permanent eclipse
behind the sparkling abyss of her pupils,
separating black from white
in a dazzling hoop
like a half-sucked lifesaver.

Her lips broke and released her confident smile.
And from behind that grin,
was warm, invisible laughter
that floated into the moonlight.

A black swan playing in the snow;
a blue flower in a red bouquet:
he couldn't tell if they were alone,
because she was all he could see.

DAYDREAM

Blue socks and black hair;
a necklace made of perfume.
I remember her now.
I can see her somehow,
with my eyes closed
in my room.

But there is more.
Unlike before,
your figure standing in my door,
I feel my lips
drag along your waist.
It is surreal,
a gentle, living taste.
We tangle into touching flesh,
skin soaked with sweat,
and heartbeat breath.
Too real to be true.
Time to wake up.

LUNCH-BREAK

While eating a chili-cheese hot dog,
he philosophically dwells on the nature of conformity,
concluding, silently:

"It is not a decision of whether to conform or not, but
rather, a goal to have as much fun as possible under the
illusion of conformity."

Shit.

He notices he has gotten a chili stain
on his designer jeans.

KNIGHT ON A STICK HORSE

A short compliment
could not possibly say
enough.

Wait.

A long compliment
may reveal too much.

Red-handed, he surmised,
he thinks about her more than he should.

A PARTY FAVOR

A *knock-knock-knock*
around eleven o'clock.
To his surprise, you opened it.

Seeing your dark locks
struck him like writer's block,
and he couldn't shape his tongue
to use it.

Submerged in words, but unable to find
the ones that don't pronounce:

"I need you."

PRECIPITATION & PERCEPTION

A cold and rainy February.
He is walking alone.
Smiling, dry, and warm
in the surrogate embrace
of your big, yellow raincoat.

WANDERLUST

My eyes look for your smile.
My ears listen for your voice.
My lips wonder what they've missed,
as my thoughts chase my memories of you
around my mind.

They deliver me serenity,
carried on the winds of memories.
I see giggling, flickering photographs.
And for a moment,
I'm filled with the sense
that you were just here.

IN CONCERT TOGETHER

I'm just a face in a crowd
looking at thousands of faces.
To face reality is to face my fears.
Gutless, I look away.
Just a face in a crowd;
drifting in circles to avoid my problems.
But my worries are in your background,
in this crowd
surrounded by sound.
You're looking at these faces, too.
I feel like a shadow,
as I stand quietly behind you,
wondering to myself, *how I could live without you?*
What can I do?
But then, you turn,
smiling, to tell me,
"Look at these people
with their many, different faces,
in this sea."
And I grin, too,
but the only face I can see
is you.

SOUND CHECKS

It was twelve o'clock; well, right around.
Everyone was ready for the band from out of town,
"Check! Check!" He is loud and clear.
The song starts. The crowd begins to cheer.
"What, dear?" The dark-haired Cinderella came near,
"It's so loud in here. You'll have to speak in my ear!"

What the fuck should I say?
he thinks, looking at her rear.
The smell of crab-apples grabs him,
her perfume, with a touch of beer
rushing to his head, forgetting his fear.
His heart is pounding.
He wants to be sincere.
His eyes follow the line
from her cheek to the base of her neck,
where the waterfall of her midnight hair
cascades into her ivory skin.

He says, "I'll tell you later. It's really loud."

LAST CALL FOR FEAR

It was an empty, brown-bottle beer stare
closing the distance from here to there.
His mind wandering everywhere.
If it was time to be right or wrong,
she hadn't decided till that last song.
He loved the way her body moved and bent;
that present, so pleasant.
To their future, together they went.
Here to there,
like yes and no.
Choose one, then go,
because the other choice,
no one will ever know.

BODY LANGUAGE

It was the "oh"
in their hello.
The drinks were
just a show.
It was the lips
of his fingertips
that spoke lust
against the curve of her hips.
It was the "why"
in his good-bye,
from tired pillow eyes
and drunken lies.
It was the repose
of her tiptoes
through scattered clothes:
what she never said,
what he didn't know.

GOOD MOURNING

I am dreaming.
Wake me to talk,
or leave me while I sleep.
Please, do not wake me to go.
Just leave me here,
dreaming of you.

BYGONE

You say nothing before the morning comes,
because today,
you are gone.
The mourning comes when I know:
it wasn't really you
there in my dreams;
but the real memory of your smile,
alive, inside of me.

HE FINDS OUT ABOUT HIM

He understood every word
between the two love birds,
and he was the third.
Sitting in an empty, white room,
buried in an avalanche of thoughts,
every moment was a waste;
a bitter after-taste.
Thinking of every sweet phrase,
reliving every gaze,
retracing the maze...

Sitting in a lockless cage,
too scared to turn the page.

THE DECISION

A hungry romance, or a well-fed lie,
he holds a yellow daffodil against a periwinkle sky,
then picks the petals and lets them fly;
not quite ready to say good-bye.

Thinking of how she loved him,
then, on second thought,
how she loved him not.

THEIR FINAL DATE

On the last morning of winter,
her six A.M. silhouette
blurred in his sleepy eyes.

In the last minutes of winter,
their breath and their silence
gave quiet good-byes.

With the last seconds of winter,
the door shut,
the clock ticked,
and he realized:

even the saddest rhyming words
would never bring her back.

HER LAST WORDS

Waiting for your words,
the closing door states:
"There isn't anymore."

A DAY LATER

The words she spoke just to keep talking
were the ideas
and the presence
that crystalized him.
He could not speak,
nor could he hear.
Solidified by his desire,
he did not care.
Finally broken by the light of truth,
left only to sit and stare.
Too scared to turn away,
because every shard left that day
still sparkled in front of his eyes
in exactly the same way.

A WEEK LATER

He fell a step behind, or maybe two.
But in that moment,
he saw something completely new.
"Stop,"
he asked, "look at this view!"
But his shtick was not your glue.

So he got left standing still;
still behind you.
He watched you fade away
only to say,
"Good-bye,"
to his beautiful view
of a world with you.

ACCEPTANCE

Limbo to vertigo,
she floated above
while he walked below.
It was a new angle:
a human turning into an angel.

Strolling through the air,
the wind in her hair;
it was more than he could bear.
Here, then there.
She would fly away.
Despite his best gimmicks,
she'd never stay.

Not given the time to talk,
he failed to stand,
then forgot how to walk.

At forty-five past eleven,
on a cold day in heaven,
he could tell, quite well:
this was not the paradise he'd imagined,
but a very chilly hell.

DEPRESSION

Hollow as an echo:
he wonders where his thoughts go.

Living, dying, and immortal in their time,
but removed from him,
never left to be.
Drowned in the memory
of her sea.

He wishes for new thoughts.
As an empty tunnel
waiting anxiously for the next train
to pass through him and give life.
A rush of purpose.

Because with nowhere to run
and nothing to run from,
he is stuck on this track
dwelling on this fact:
there is no one around to tell him
that he is not alone.

.

HIS FIRE

The timber laid in front of his head,
He sat watching as the fire quietly spread.

He thought about you
while he watched the wood burn.
He thought about love
as he watched the colors turn.

With brilliant colors, it crept across,
burning heat, then the flame was lost.
Blackened on the other side,
smoldering with sadness, jealousy, and pride.

Until all that was has burned away,
we pay the price of fire play.

HER SEA

It was overcast on the shore of your sea.
I thought I saw you drowning,
and no one to save you except for me.

Then, I jumped into that ocean
so you could see,
truly, what a hero I could be.

Fighting the currents gave me strength;
it was like my hero's cape.
But from the undertow, I couldn't escape.

Tossed and tossed incessantly,
tossed and tossed into insanity.

My wife? My sister? My friend? My lover?
My home? My accomplice? My queen? My mother?

Who was it drowning in your sea?

Was it ever you?
Was it only me?

THE RESOLUTION

This was my final farewell to thee.
So, before I go peacefully,
please tell me where to place our memories.
There are so many that I cannot just be;
the sound of your laughter still ringing inside of me.

The cute way you wore your hair,
it made me stare.
Your skin was soft and fair.
A personality with eccentric flair.
Since you didn't care,
I carried this fantasy with me everywhere.

Whether or not you did see:
you were weathering me.
As we walked on the sand,
but did not touch the sea,
I let go of your hand,
but did not feel free.
Why did we find this lock,
only to throw away the key?

Uncertainty
was blurring me.

One eye cried,
while the other lied.
Like Dr. Jekyll and Mr. Hyde,
my soul was caught in a divide
between yours and my side.

Night to night, my life skipped the sun;
a waltz of *what if's* that made me numb.
Almost there, but never won.
Circles of nothing
I decided to run,
and *it* was done.

I was like the desert
thinking about the rain.
For a moment, I was soaked
with all of its joy and pain.

A moment later, I would be a wasteland again.
But as we stood,
one last time,
in the summer snow; juxtaposed,
we joked about the hot and cold,
growing up and growing old.

I saw the magic that love foretold:
how it lives in the hearts
of the hands that we hold.

That the good and love did not go in vain.
True hands always remain,
because good will is what they contain.

So, I stopped thinking like I was the desert,
and started living like I was the rain.

In the wasteland, I could not hide,
with eyes opened wide.

Plenty of time to live for those who have died.
To watch the past and present collide,
and end up on the brighter side.

FREEDOM

D
 A
N
 G
L
 E
 D

from
the
cord
of
Expectations.

Snap!

Let down.
Pain.
Confusion.
Freedom.

ABOUT THE AUTHOR

Bart is a New York native, artist, and author. He has written three major literary works and completed hundreds of pieces of art and featured in numerous solo exhibitions over his time spent at home and abroad in Europe. He has his master's degree in Public Administration and makes his career as a professional city planner. Bart rides his longboard everywhere and enjoys making art, music, and playing video games with friends in his spare time.